ALLIES

Also by Alan Gratz

Grenade
Refugee

ALAN GRATZ

ALLIES

 SCHOLASTIC

Scholastic Children's Books
An imprint of Scholastic Ltd
Euston House, 24 Eversholt Street, London, NW1 1DB, UK
Registered office: Westfield Road, Southam, Warwickshire, CV47 0RA
SCHOLASTIC and associated logos are trademarks and/or
registered trademarks of Scholastic Inc.

First published in the US by Scholastic Inc, 2019
First published in the UK by Scholastic Ltd, 2019

ISBN 978 1407 19879 8

A CIP catalogue record for this book
is available from the British Library.

Printed by CPI Group (UK) Ltd, Croydon, CR0 4YY
Papers used by Scholastic Children's Books are made
from wood grown in sustainable forests.

1 3 5 7 9 10 8 6 4 2

www.scholastic.co.uk

For my longtime ally
Paul Harrill

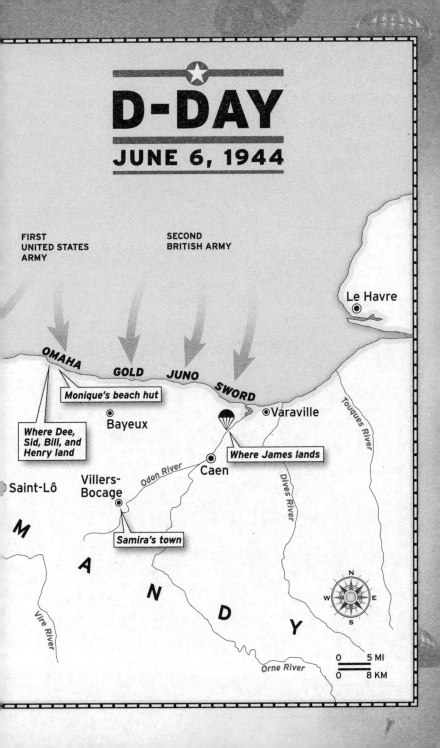

D-DAY
JUNE 6, 1944

FIRST
UNITED STATES
ARMY

SECOND
BRITISH ARMY

Le Havre

OMAHA

GOLD   JUNO   SWORD

Monique's beach hut

Varaville

Bayeux

Where Dee,
Sid, Bill, and
Henry land

Touques River

Where James lands

Odon River   Caen

Saint-Lô

Villers-
Bocage

Dives River

M

Samira's town

A

N

D

Y

Vire River

N

W   E

S

0   5 MI

0   8 KM

Orne River

Soldiers, Sailors and Airmen of the Allied Expeditionary Force!

You are about to embark upon the Great Crusade, toward which we have striven these many months. The eyes of the world are upon you. The hopes and prayers of liberty-loving people everywhere march with you. In company with our brave Allies and brothers-in-arms on other Fronts, you will bring about the destruction of the German war machine, the elimination of Nazi tyranny over the oppressed peoples of Europe, and security for ourselves in a free world.

—General Dwight D. Eisenhower, Order of the Day, June 6, 1944

OPERATION NEPTUNE

JUNE 6, 1944

JUST BEFORE DAWN

ON THE ENGLISH CHANNEL

A-HUNTING WE WILL GO

Dee Carpenter's foot slipped off the wet ladder and his stomach lurched into his throat. He scrabbled for a handhold, but the weight of his pack and his rifle dragged him down. At the same instant, a gap opened up between the huge transport ship he was leaving and the little motorboat he was supposed to be climbing into. Dee dropped like a stone toward the cold black water of the English Channel.

A hand shot out and caught the pack on Dee's back. Dee jolted, then swung into the side of the ship with a *thump*.

"Grab on!" his friend Sid Jacobstein yelled.

With shaking, frozen hands, Dee fumbled until he was clinging to the side of the ladder.

"Legs up!" Sid told him. Dee pulled his feet up in

time to keep them from getting crushed as the motor-boat drifted back to *clang* against the side of the transport ship.

Dee took a deep breath and closed his eyes in relief.

"For crying out loud, Dee, you just about killed yourself before the Germans could do it for you," Sid said.

Sid had been right below Dee on the ladder, and now they were face-to-face. With his free hand, Dee grabbed Sid's shoulder.

"Thanks, Sid," he said, still panting. "I owe you one."

"Private Carpenter! Private Jacobstein! If you two knuckleheads are done fooling around, we've got a boat to load," Sergeant Taylor called from above.

Dee and Sid helped each other climb into the small boat. They took their places halfway back, in a row of other soldiers wearing olive-green assault jackets and green metal helmets.

Though they wore the same uniform, Dee and Sid couldn't have resembled each other less. Dee was sixteen and looked even younger. He had spindly arms and legs, and he worried that his baggy green army trousers made him look like a child playing soldier. Sid was just a year older, but he was six feet, four inches tall and built like Hank Greenberg, the big power-hitting left fielder for the Detroit Tigers. He could have bent Dee into a pretzel if he'd wanted to. Sid had a long face, curly brown hair, tan skin, and stubble on his jaw. Dee was blond-haired and pale-skinned, and he couldn't grow a mustache if his life depended on it.

What had first united them was their shared hatred of the New York Yankees. Sid was a die-hard Brooklyn Dodgers fan, while Dee rooted for his hometown baseball team, the Philadelphia Athletics.

"The Dodgers'll be back in the World Series as soon as the war's over. You'll see," Sid said to Dee, continuing a conversation that had begun on the troop transport ship. "Of course they had an off season last year. Half the team enlisted to fight."

Another soldier overheard him. "Are you kiddin'?" he said. His New York accent was even stronger than Sid's. "The Yankees lost as many players—*including* Joe DiMaggio—and they won the pennant *and* the World Series!"

How Sid or any of the rest of them could think about baseball right now—could think about *anything* besides their impending doom—astounded Dee. He staggered on the metal deck as the boat rocked from side to side on the waves, and Sid steadied him to keep him from falling.

They were in one of the famous Higgins boats that Dee had heard about, but it wasn't much to look at. It was basically a big metal bathtub with a motor at the back and a tall door at the front. But Dee knew that its flat bottom was what made the boat special; it allowed the boat to run right up onto a beach, drop the front door, deliver its forty passengers, then back out, reload, and make another run.

It was this Higgins boat that would deliver Dee and Sid and the rest of their platoon to Omaha Beach in Normandy, France.

The Allied invasion of Europe was about to begin.

Since the war started five years ago, Nazi Germany had rolled across Europe, blitzing through Poland and the Netherlands and Belgium and France. Now the map that had hung in Dee's high school history classroom back in Philadelphia was all wrong. Instead of a bunch of different-colored countries in Europe, there was just one big red blob—Germany—covering everything. And if Germany's demented leader Adolf Hitler and his armies had their way, that big red blob would grow and grow and grow until it covered the whole *world*.

Unless Dee and everyone else here put a stop to it.

Dee couldn't see over the top of the Higgins boat's high walls, but he knew how many other ships were out there on the water. He'd seen them gathered last night, at what the British sailors on his transport ship had dubbed "Piccadilly Circus," after a famous traffic intersection in London. Hundreds of ships. *Thousands*. Transport ships. Destroyers. Battleships as long as skyscrapers turned on their sides. Minesweepers dragging the sea for German mines. And more that Dee couldn't even identify. Their lights had glittered like stars in the night.

There at Piccadilly Circus, where the ships had all come together, Dee and Sid had been up on the top deck when they heard a Scottish soldier on a British ship belt out "The Road to the Isles" on his bagpipes. The piper got laughs and applause from all the other soldiers waiting on their transports, and more GIs on Dee's ship came up from below to listen. Not to be outdone, a United States battleship broadcast "God Bless America" over its loudspeakers, and Dee and Sid and the boys around them whooped. A Free French ship played "La Marseillaise," the national anthem of the country they had lost and were going back to reclaim, and Dee got chills. Sailors on a Canadian ship joined in with "O Canada," and some Australian soldiers sang "Waltzing Matilda." There were more songs too—songs in Polish and Norwegian and Dutch—so many that Dee couldn't hear them all at once.

An English ship had capped it all off by playing a recording of "A-Hunting We Will Go" and gotten the biggest cheer of them all.

But nobody was cheering now, and no one was singing. Sid wasn't even talking baseball anymore. They had all grown quiet as the remainder of their platoon climbed down from the transport ship into the Higgins boat. It was still dark out, and they couldn't see France, couldn't tell how far away they were from shore. But suddenly they were hit with the cold, hard reality that *it* was finally about to happen. After months of training, months of planning, months of waiting, Dee and Sid and everyone else—more than *a hundred and fifty thousand* soldiers—were about to be delivered right into the jaws of death.

Today was D-Day. The most important day of the Second World War. Maybe the most important day in all of human history. Dee got goose bumps just thinking about it. Everything was riding on this day.

If they screwed it up, the world would never be the same.

The weight of the moment pushed down on Dee and the others. The dull, heavy sound of the small boat clanging against the side of the transport ship sounded like a church bell, tolling their deaths.

"Word is, anywhere from a quarter of us to a half of us are gonna die before we ever get off the beach," Sid said.

Dee's stomach tightened. They'd all heard those

same odds. They all knew that when they landed on the beach, the German army would be waiting for them with machine guns and mortars and mines. Dee glanced around. Even the veterans among them—the guys in their twenties who had fought in Algeria and Italy and other places—even they were silent, sinking into whatever lonely thoughts a man thinks in the hours before he might die.

A soldier behind Sid gave him a shove. "Not such a big man now, are you, yid?" he sneered.

Dee felt Sid tense up beside him. *Yid* was a slur for a Jewish person, and Sid was the only Jewish guy in their platoon. The fact that his first name rhymed with *yid* had made it his nickname since boot camp.

"You'd think he'd be happy," another soldier said. "Always talking about killing Krauts." *Krauts*, along with *Jerries*, was a word a lot of them used for the Germans. "But Sid the Yid's just as scared as the rest of us."

Ever since he'd arrived at boot camp, if Sid wasn't talking about the Dodgers, he was talking about killing Germans. Lots of soldiers were here because they'd been drafted. The guys who'd volunteered, they usually did it for things like patriotism, or glory, or to have a steady job. But Dee knew that, for Sid, the war in Germany was personal. For years now, the Nazis had been rounding up the Jews of Europe and taking everything they owned and making them into slaves.

Sid was out for revenge.

Dee turned to face the soldiers who were ragging on Sid. "Leave him alone," Dee said.

One of the soldiers laughed. "The yid can't even fight his own fights!"

Dee saw Sid's fists clench. Sid was half a head taller than either of the other soldiers and had fifty pounds on each of them, but he didn't take a swing. Sid and Dee both knew what happened when a Jewish guy punched somebody for insulting him. They'd seen it happen again and again in basic training. It was the Jew who got in trouble, not the other guy.

"I'm saving it for the Krauts, fathead," Sid said. "I'm gonna kill the first German I see, and then every single Kraut I meet from Normandy to Berlin."

The two soldiers shook their heads and looked away. Sid nodded his thanks to Dee for sticking up for him, but it didn't make Dee feel better. In fact, it made him feel worse.

Sid was Dee's best friend in the army. His only friend. They knew almost everything there was to know about each other, except the one big, giant thing that Dee had hidden from Sid and the rest of the men in his platoon.

Everybody called him "Dee" because that was the

first letter of the name on his dog tags: *D. Carpenter.* Short for Douglas Carpenter. But what Sid and the others didn't know—could never know—was that Douglas Carpenter wasn't Dee's real name at all.

His real name was Dietrich Zimmermann, and he was German.

NIGHT AND FOG

The last of the soldiers climbed down into the Higgins boat, and the motor revved.

"All right, you grunts!" Sergeant Taylor shouted from the front, over the noise of the motor. "Here we go!"

Dee closed his eyes as the small boat moved away from the transport ship, and he remembered the day that his journey to this moment began.

It was the summer of 1943. The Philadelphia Athletics were twenty-six games behind the Yankees. The Japanese had bombed Pearl Harbor less than two years ago, Germany had declared war soon after, and the United States was in full-on battle mode. The Philadelphia Navy Yard was building battleships, Groucho Marx was on the radio telling everyone to buy war bonds, and Dietrich Zimmermann was about to become Douglas Carpenter.

Dee sat in a creaky wooden chair in the office of a US Army recruiter in Philadelphia, wringing his hands in his lap. He wanted to throw up. It was over ninety degrees outside, and a rattling electric fan blew the hot air around the room. Sweat ran down Dee's back and collected at his waistline. A poster on the wall with a picture of Uncle Sam rolling up his sleeves for a fight read DEFEND YOUR COUNTRY! ENLIST NOW IN THE UNITED STATES ARMY!

Dee wanted to do just that, but he was afraid he was going to be busted. Yes, he'd been born in Germany— but that wasn't what he was trying to hide. It was right there on his birth certificate. He was an "enemy alien." But there were plenty of foreign nationals fighting for the United States in the army. The real problem was, Dee was just sixteen.

You could enlist in the United States Army on your own at eighteen, and with your parents' permission at seventeen. To enlist at sixteen, you had to fudge your birth certificate and find a recruiter willing to look the other way. Otherwise, you could end up in jail for lying on your enlistment papers. But the US Army needed every able body they could get, and Dee knew two other boys from his class who'd been able to join up. He hoped the same would hold true for him.

The recruitment officer was a short man with wide shoulders and a flat face. The nameplate on his desk said he was Captain Graham. Dee swallowed and sat up tall, trying to look bigger. Captain Graham studied Dee for a moment, then reached for his stamp. *Thump-thump*. Dee was officially 1-A: Available and fit for military service.

Dee let out a breath. He was in the army!

"Your parents' status as political refugees means you'll most likely be on a watch list in Germany," the captain said. "I'll put you in the Pacific, fighting Japan, so you're not in danger of getting caught."

"No!" Dee said, louder and more forcefully than he'd meant to. He tried to calm down. "No, sir. I'd like to go back to Germany, sir. I want to beat Hitler."

Captain Graham nodded. "I get it, kid. I can send you there, get you in on a division likely to see action in France, when it comes. But maybe you don't want to go back as Dietrich Zimmermann."

Dee didn't understand.

"We get lots of recruits the Germans don't like," said Captain Graham. "Poles, Czechs, Slavs, Austrians, French, Italians. Most of them are Jews, but a few of them are political enemies of Germany, like your family. In some cases, we change their names on their paperwork and their dog tags so the Germans won't know who they are if they're caught. So Dietrich becomes . . . say, Douglas. And your last name, Zimmermann, becomes—"

"Carpenter," Dee said. "That's what Zimmermann means in German. Carpenter."

Which was how Douglas Carpenter was born.

The US government knew Dee's real name and where he was born, but no one else did. Not even his commanding officer. And especially not Sid.

On the Higgins boat, Dee heard a soldier behind him throw up, and he was dragged revoltingly back to the here and now. Another soldier in front of Dee vomited into the inch of seawater that had already gathered at the bottom of the Higgins boat. The boat was rocking back and forth on the waves, and Dee could feel himself turning green with seasickness too. He instantly regretted the corned beef he'd eaten for breakfast. Sid gave him a reassuring smile and Dee fought down the bile in his throat.

High up in the sky, Dee heard the drone of airplanes. Dozens of them. He looked up, but he couldn't see anything for the clouds.

"Bombers?" Dee asked Sid.

Sid shook his head. "Paratroopers."

One of the vets in their row nodded. "Our part, Operation Neptune, storming the beach at Normandy," he shouted, "that's just one piece of the whole big Operation Overlord. There's lots of other stuff going on right now, this very second. Other operations and missions. Gliders delivering guns and soldiers. Paratroopers capturing bridges and roads. French Resistance fighters taking out communications so the Nazis can't call for reinforcements after we land. Any one of those operations fail, and it won't matter which of us lives and which of us dies on those beaches."

Dee swallowed hard. They weren't landing on the beach just yet, he reminded himself. They were still waiting for the hundreds of other Higgins boats to be loaded. Then they would all go in together at dawn.

Overhead, clouds engulfed the full moon and a thick fog rolled in. *Night and fog.* With a shiver, Dee remembered something else. An older memory, from when he was a little boy in Germany.

On a night just like this, when Dee was five years old, his uncle Otto had disappeared from his home and was never seen or heard from again. Otto had been a labor leader, helping factory workers come together as unions to demand better working conditions and better pay. But the Nazis didn't like unions and liked union leaders even less. So the Nazis had come for Uncle Otto in the night and taken him. Nothing in his home had been touched or broken, and no authority claimed to know where he was. There was no one to complain to. No one to petition. To this day, Dee and his parents had no idea where Uncle Otto might be, if he was in a prison or a concentration camp, alive or dead. It was as though Uncle Otto had simply ceased to exist. The Nazis could do that: erase you from existence. The Germans had an expression for people disappearing at night into the fog of the Nazi political machine: *Nacht und Nebel*. Night and Fog.

Uncle Otto's disappearance was the final straw for Dee's parents. They'd already been horrified by the Nazis' growing power in their country. Stunned by how many people voted for the Nazis and showed up at their rallies. Nazi flags had appeared on every office building and shop and home, until it became dangerous *not* to have one. Until dissent became unpatriotic. Until it became criminal to not stand and salute the führer.

And the worst part was that Germany hadn't suddenly "become" racist and evil. That rot had been there, under the surface, the whole time. Hitler's hate-filled speeches had allowed the seeds of German bigotry to grow like weeds until they choked out anything else that might have flowered there. Dee and his family had just been living in their own little bubble and hadn't noticed it.

But they saw it clearly when Uncle Otto disappeared into the Night and Fog. They left Germany while they still could, before the war started. They came to America as refugees, and Dee's new life in Philadelphia began at age five.

The Higgins boat was slapped by a giant wave, and the cold water made Dee gasp. Seawater was pouring in over the side of the boat. Too much water. Sergeant

Taylor barked orders for everyone to bail. Dee looked around for a bucket, but there weren't any nearby. Beside him, Sid pulled off his helmet, gave Dee a grin and a shrug, and scooped his helmet into the vomit-filled water at their feet. Dee did the same, tossing a helmetful of sick-stew over the side.

Would Sid care that Dee's parents had disagreed with Hitler? Would Sid care that they had run away to America so Dee wouldn't be scooped up by the Hitler Youth and brainwashed to hate everyone who wasn't a "pure" German? That Dee had been in America for almost his whole life, so long that he had lost any trace of his German accent?

Or would Sid blame Dee and his parents for what had happened in Germany? It was true that Dee's family hadn't been the ones persecuting Jews and other minorities. But Dee and his parents hadn't done anything to try to stop the Nazis either. They hadn't spoken up when they could, and when it was too late to speak up, they had run away.

Somewhere beyond the fog, the sun broke the horizon. Dee felt the rumble of the boat's motor in the pit of his stomach, and he realized they were heading toward the shore.

They were going in to land on Omaha Beach at last.

DEE-DAY

Fa-FOOM.

Dee flinched and ducked. One of the big American destroyers behind his Higgins boat fired all its guns at once, shelling the German defenses on shore. The huge shells felt like a freight train roaring past. Battleships up and down the line fired again and again, their muzzles flashing bright orange in the darkness.

The Higgins boat plowed ahead through the waves, and even though it was summer, Dee was cold. The sea spray and the water at the bottom of the boat froze him to the bone. He hugged himself and crouched low, staring at the green metal helmets of the soldiers in front of him.

Nobody spoke. You couldn't. You'd have to yell to be heard over the motor, and the ocean, and the battleships, and the planes droning by overhead. Most everybody was lost in their own thoughts anyway.

Dee thought of his parents. His mother, a thin woman with long blond hair who worked as an illustrator for a pattern-design company. His father, a short, balding man who managed a food warehouse. His parents had left behind everything they knew and everyone they loved to get Dee out of Nazi Germany. They'd learned a new language and started new lives and made a new home for their son. Would he ever see them again?

Dee felt a tear run down his cheek. He pretended to wipe away the sea spray as he dragged his sleeve across his face.

"Hey," Sid said to Dee, yelling right in his ear to be heard. "It's *D*-Day. Get it? *Dee*-Day. This is *your* day, Dee. That means you gotta make it through okay."

Despite the sick feeling in his stomach, Dee smiled. Every time the US Army started a mission, the first day was called D-Day. That's what the *D* stood for: It meant "Day-Day," or "Starting Day." There had been plenty of other D-Days before. But this was the big one, and all the soldiers knew it. THE D-Day.

And Dee liked the idea of this one being "Dee-Day." *His* day. It kind of was, after all. It was Dee's day for atonement. The day he came back to Europe to undo what his family had allowed to happen eleven years ago. Today was the culmination of events that had been set in motion that night Uncle Otto had disappeared.

Dee heard a scream like the squeal of a radio overhead, and he looked up. A cloud of rockets shot past, fire and smoke drawing orange and gray streaks across the sky. The rockets went on and on and on. Hundreds of them. Thousands. Dee and his platoonmates looked around at each other in wonder—this was something new.

Boom. Boom-boom-boom-boom. Dee heard the rockets explode up ahead, beyond the seven-foot-tall ramp at the front of their boat. Sid smiled at Dee, as if to say, "What could be left for us to fight after *that*?" But the grim expressions on the faces of the veterans around them dulled Dee's optimism.

At the front of the boat, Sergeant Taylor turned to yell at them.

"All right, you louts. This is it!" he shouted. "This isn't just an invasion of France. It's a toehold in Europe. The first step in pushing the Jerries all the way back to Berlin. We're the foot in the door. The wrench in the works. The kick in Hitler's nuts."

Dee sat up straighter, listening closely.

"I don't have to tell you how big this is!" the sergeant continued. "You've seen it. All the years of planning by the muckety-mucks in Washington and London. All the ships, planes, and tanks. All the pilots and spies and paratroopers and artillerymen and sailors and medics who did their part so we could be where we are, right here, right now, standing in a puddle of our own sick with Normandy and all of Europe right behind this ramp. Everything's come together for this one moment, and now it's all down to us. So don't screw it up."

Great pep talk, Sergeant, Dee thought as the Higgins boat shuddered and bumped. The engine slowed.

Sid put his helmet to Dee's helmet and bellowed in his big, deep voice, "Don't worry, buddy—we're going to get through this together!"

Then the boat hit the beach, and the ramp fell down on history.

OPERATION TORTOISE

JUNE 6, 1944

SIX HOURS BEFORE THE BEACH INVASION

NEAR VILLERS-BOCAGE, FRANCE

THE DICE ARE
ON THE CARPET

A door slammed in the sleepy French village, making eleven-year-old Samira Zidane jump. She gripped her mother's hand tighter as they hurried along the road out of town. Her mother squeezed back. *I'm scared too,* the squeeze told her, *but we'll get through this together.*

Samira's mother, Kenza Zidane, wore a tan raincoat and a blue kerchief, doing her best to hide her beauty— and her black hair and light brown skin. Samira and her mother were French Algerian, and the Nazis weren't tolerant of anyone who didn't match their white-skinned, blond-haired Aryan ideal. Samira wished she'd brought a kerchief to hide her hair and face too. But she'd gotten dressed too quickly and wore just a simple green dress and brown sweater.

Samira searched for the full moon in the sky, but clouds covered it, making the road beyond the village dark and full of shadows. It wasn't quiet though. Night was never quiet in this part of northern France. Not since the German occupation began. Night after night, American and English planes droned overhead, dropping bombs on Normandy's bigger cities. Samira had heard that Caen, Vire, and Lisieux were more rubble than buildings now. The Germans, refusing to take the beating without a fight, rattled anti-aircraft guns at the bombers, drawing brilliant white lines across the sky like fireworks.

Samira and her mother needed the noise and the darkness. It was well after curfew, when no one was allowed to be on the streets but soldiers. If you were caught out after curfew, you were automatically arrested and thrown into jail. If you were lucky. Samira had seen Germans shoot people as spies just for being out late.

And that's what Samira's mother was. A spy for the French Resistance.

Samira herself wasn't a spy, but she was a convenient prop. If caught, they had a practiced story that Samira was sick and Kenza was taking her to a doctor. That was why they were out so late at night and couldn't wait until morning. The Nazis were unlikely to be sympathetic, but at least it was a realistic excuse for why they were out when they shouldn't be. And a woman with an eleven-year-old girl in tow was far less likely to be accused of being a spy.

Samira's mother pulled her along by the hand, her eyes scanning every inch of the road and the fields. They had been out after curfew before, and it was always dangerous. But if ever there was a night to take the risk, this was it.

That evening, during the nightly BBC radio broadcast from England, Samira and her mother had heard the words all of France had been waiting to hear: *"Les dés sont sur le tapis. Il fait chaud à Suez."* "The dice are on the carpet. It's hot in Suez." They were code words. They were meaningless to the Germans, but they meant everything to the French Resistance, the scattered groups of citizens who had taken up arms and were hiding out in the forests and mountains and villages, fighting a guerrilla war against the Nazi occupation. The code words meant that the Allied forces were invading France at last.

And it was the job of Samira and her mother to take that message to the Resistance fighters south of their little town of Villers-Bocage.

As they hurried toward the woods, where their contacts in the Resistance were hiding, Samira remembered another desperate night journey with her mother: their escape from Paris four years ago. Millions of

Parisians had left the city in the days before the Nazis rolled in, but Samira's family had stayed. Her parents were students from Algeria at the University of Paris, and they had nowhere else to go. Samira had watched in horror as the Nazi soldiers goose-stepped their way down the Champs-Élysées, Paris's famous avenue of shops, theaters, and cafés. The Nazis had hung their swastika flag from the Arc de Triomphe and filled the Parisian cafés like they were on holiday.

Samira's parents were in favor of Algerian independence from France, but with the Nazis in control, they knew that dream would never come true. So in 1940, Samira's father had taken part in a student protest against the German occupation. But the Nazis did not take kindly to protests. In the massacre that followed, German soldiers killed Samira's father. Samira had been just seven years old. Fearing for their lives, Samira's mother had fled with her from Paris into the countryside, aided by a fledgling Resistance group made up of former students turned rebels. Here, among the farms and hedgerows of Normandy, using false papers to hide their identities, Samira and her mother had survived.

They had worked as messengers for the Resistance ever since.

Samira and her mother were almost in the woods when they heard shouting and crying from up the road.

Samira's heartbeat quickened. Trouble? Here in the countryside? This late at night?

Samira and her mother ducked into the cover of blueberry bushes beside the road. They crept along until they saw a group of farmhouses where French families were being dragged from their homes and loaded into trucks at gunpoint by soldiers.

Nazi soldiers.

Samira watched the raid from the shadows, her pulse pounding in her ears.

"When will you learn?" a Nazi officer said to the French farmers in heavily accented French. "For every one of us you kill, a hundred of you will die!"

"This must be retaliation for the killing of Major Vogel," Samira's mother whispered. The Nazi officer had been murdered by the French Resistance less than a day ago. "I've told them not to do that. They'll only send another Nazi bigwig, and we always pay heavily for it."

"But we did nothing!" cried one of the old men being dragged from his home. "None of us was responsible!"

Samira knew it didn't matter. This was standard operating procedure for the Nazis. If one of their men was assassinated, they took their revenge by rounding up a hundred of the local French citizens and executing them publicly. Her heart went out to the French farmers. None of this was their fault, but they were the ones being punished.

A flash of movement behind one of the farmhouses caught Samira's attention.

"*Look,*" she whispered to her mother, pointing. A woman was lifting her young children out of a ground-floor window to escape from the Nazis.

"We have to help her," Samira's mother said. She was already standing to go to the woman's aid.

"But what about the radio message?" Samira asked. "What if we're caught?"

"We're in the Resistance, Samira," her mother told her. "We resist."

IN THE DOGHOUSE

As Samira and her mother ran to help the woman and her children, a little white dog on a rope in the backyard started to bark excitedly.

"Samira," her mother whispered, "see what you can do to get that dog quiet."

Samira ran for the dog. It leaped up on her happily, tail wagging, and licked her face.

"Yes! Yes. Hello, dog," Samira said. "We need to be quiet now so the Nazis don't catch us."

It was too late. German soldiers came around the side of the house with rifles in hand, and they caught the French woman and Samira's mother as they were taking the last of four children out of the window.

Samira's breath caught in her throat, and her heart stopped. *Maman!* she thought. *No!*

The soldiers yelled orders in German while the

French mother begged for her children's lives. Kenza Zidane gave her daughter a look laced with fear, and Samira clapped her hand around the little dog's snout and backed into its doghouse, where she was swallowed in shadow. Samira watched, tears streaming down her face, as one of the soldiers yanked off her mother's beautiful blue kerchief and tossed it on the ground before dragging her away along with the French family.

"Don't come after me, Samira!" her mother called out in Arabic, knowing the German guards wouldn't understand. "Get somewhere safe and stay there! I will see you again in heaven, love of my heart!"

Samira hiccuped a sob and put a hand over her own mouth so she wouldn't cry out. Tears streamed down her face. *Maman!*

The little dog in Samira's arms started growling, and there was nothing she could do to quiet him. One of the soldiers turned at the sound and started walking toward the doghouse. Samira shook with fright. If the Nazi caught her, she would be reunited with her mother. Yes, she longed for that—but they would be reunited only until both of them were shot later that morning. Free, Samira could find help. Try to save her mother in time.

The soldier came closer. The little dog fought to break free of Samira's arms. The Nazi was almost on top of her now. He was bending down.

Inside, Samira screamed, *What do I do?*

UNLEASHED

Samira let go of the dog and out he bounded, barking his little head off and charging the soldier like a bull. The soldier was so surprised he cried out and stumbled back, falling down on his bottom in the dirt.

A few paces away, another Nazi soldier laughed. The little dog barked and snarled, and as he jumped around the fallen soldier, the German got tangled up in the dog's rope. That only made the other soldier laugh harder, which the fallen soldier didn't seem to appreciate. Samira held deathly still as the fallen Nazi kicked at the little dog and stood. He said something harsh to the other soldier as he untangled himself. Then he backed away, out of the range of the little dog's rope, and aimed his rifle at the dog.

No!

Samira almost said it out loud, and she had to catch

herself before leaping out to protect the dog. She didn't want to get caught, but she didn't want the dog to die either.

The other soldier said something serious through his trailing laughter. Maybe he was trying to tell the humiliated solider not to shoot the dog? But the little dog kept barking, and the soldier kept his gun aimed right in its face.

Samira couldn't take it. She couldn't let the soldier shoot the dog, even if it meant being captured herself. She crawled forward on her hands and knees. Her head had just emerged from the doghouse when—

Honk-honk!

The German truck honking in the road made both the soldiers turn and look. The truck must have been leaving, because both soldiers suddenly ran, not wanting to miss their ride back to Bayeux. Samira ducked inside the doghouse and waited until the sound of the truck was long gone before she came out again.

The little dog met her at the entrance and licked her face.

Samira wiped her eyes dry. "You almost got us both into a lot of trouble," she told the little dog. His tail wagged again, the threat of the soldiers in his yard already a distant memory. "Here. No sense leaving you tied up, now that your family is gone," Samira said. She untied the rope around the dog's collar, but he hardly seemed to notice. He was happy to sniff around her feet.

Samira went to where her mother's kerchief lay on the ground and picked it up. It was the only thing she had left of her now. Samira wrapped the kerchief around her head, tying it at the bottom, and wiped tears from her eyes again.

Enough crying. Her mother had told her to get somewhere safe and stay there. There were a dozen places Samira knew she could go and find refuge for at least the night.

But she wasn't going to do what her mother told her. She was going to do the exact *opposite*. Samira had already lost her father to the Nazis, and she wasn't going to lose her mother too.

Samira was going to free her mother. And the only way to do that was to find the Maquis.

THE BEST ACTRESS
IN HER CLASS

The Maquis would help Samira free her mother. They had to.

The "Maquis" was what everyone called the Resistance fighters. That's who Samira and her mother had been going to warn about the coming invasion in the first place. The word *maquis* meant a "bush" or "thicket" in French. Since that was where the fighters often operated from, it had come to be their name too. Taking on the German army head-to-head was suicide, so the Maquis used guerrilla tactics: attacking tanks just long enough to blow up their treads and then running away, sabotaging phone lines, blowing up weapons depots.

And assassinating German officers. Like the one for which the Nazis had been rounding people up in revenge. It was the Maquis's fault Samira's mother and the other families had been taken prisoner. That's why they had to help.

The little white dog from the house still jogged along with Samira, half following, half leading her, and always tripping her up if she wasn't watching carefully.

"*Go. Scat,*" she whispered at the dog. "*I need to hurry.*"

Samira didn't have a watch, but she knew it must be close to the time she and her mother were supposed to meet up with the Maquis in the woods. Any later than that, and the Resistance fighters would be gone. They were always on the move so the Germans couldn't find them. They would be at the rendezvous point for fifteen minutes. No more.

The dog made Samira trip again, and she huffed in frustration. She picked up a stick from the side of the road. "Go on. Get," she said. She threw the stick into the trees as far as she could, and the little dog tore off after it.

Samira had made it only a few steps before the dog came bounding back with the stick, happier than before.

It was going to be harder to get rid of this dog than Samira thought.

"All right. You can come along," she told the dog quietly. "I suppose both of us need to get our families back."

Samira adjusted her mother's kerchief around her

head, sticking to the hedgerows just off the road in case a German car happened past. There was a time back in Paris, Samira remembered, when she had always covered her hair with a headscarf.

Algeria was a colony of France, but they wanted to be their own country. That was why Samira's parents had come to France in the first place—to learn all they could about medicine and law and then return to their homeland and work for independence. Samira believed in the cause too, and to show her own nationalistic and religious pride, she had worn a headscarf to her all-girls school in Paris.

But some of the other girls—French girls—hadn't liked her independent streak, and one day their taunting had turned into a full-on fight. Samira was called to the headmistress's office, where she expected to learn the other girls were going to be punished. Instead, she found *herself* in trouble while the French girls got only a slap on the wrist.

"But I didn't start it! They did!" Samira had protested.

"You brought it on yourself, wearing that headscarf," the headmistress said. "From now on, headscarves will no longer be permitted here at Marie Curie, do you understand?"

"But there's no law against it!" Samira said.

"There is now. I am the law at this school, and I

forbid it," the headmistress said. "And if I may say so, this is precisely why you and your kind continue to be held back. Because you attempt to maintain your own identity rather than integrate into French society."

Samira's fists clenched in her lap, and she shook with anger and frustration. Everyone in France said this, but how were Algerians supposed to be French when French landlords wouldn't let them live in their buildings? When French shopkeepers wouldn't hire them? When French policemen harassed them in the streets? Algerians weren't Algerian, because there *was* no Algeria. But they weren't French citizens either. They were caught in a no-man's-land, neither one nor the other, and it was no different for Samira here at school.

"How can I 'integrate' when the school won't let me?" she asked.

"'Won't let you'? Nonsense," said the headmistress. "Every opportunity open to the other girls at Marie Curie is open to you."

"But is that really true?" Samira asked. Years of pent-up frustration were finally bubbling over, and she picked just the latest indignity she had suffered. "I am the best actress in my class by far, and yet I have never once been cast in the school play. Why? Because I'm Algerian?"

"Of course not," the headmistress said. "There are just no parts for a girl who is . . ."

"Brown?" Samira finished for her.

The headmistress's face seemed to grow darker before Samira's eyes. "I cannot help it if all of the great works of theater in the last two millennia have been written by Europeans," the headmistress said coldly.

"There are girls playing the parts of *boys*," Samira pointed out, "but a brown girl can't play a character whose skin color isn't even mentioned?"

The headmistress lowered her eyelids at her. "Perhaps, Miss Zidane, you didn't get a role in the play because you are not quite the actress you think you are."

Samira broke down in tears, blubbering about her insecurities and failings. The headmistress's tone quickly shifted to one of sympathy and regret, and she hurried around her desk to comfort Samira.

"I'm so sorry, my dear," the headmistress said. "Perhaps I could speak to Ms. Dumont. Find a small role for you somewhere."

Samira stopped crying as suddenly as she had begun, her face snapping back to normal. She had only been acting upset.

"No thank you, headmistress," she said, rising calmly to leave. "I think I will wait for a part that matches the level of my talent."

The little dog growled, bringing Samira back to the present and the dark, cool Normandy night. Her furry friend had sensed them before Samira had seen them.

Two Nazi soldiers, guarding the bridge up ahead.

LITTLE LOST DOG

Samira picked up the dog and backed into a hedgerow on the edge of a cherry orchard. German soldiers? Here on the bridge? It was a short bridge, but it was the only way across the swift, deep river.

Samira's mind spun. She had to meet with the Maquis. Tonight. She had to get them to free her mother and the others from the German prison before they were killed. There wasn't time to walk along the river, looking for another bridge. But she couldn't just walk past the guards either.

Samira spied an abandoned cherry basket at the base of a tree, and an idea came to her.

"I'm going to need your help," she told the dog. "But you're not going to like the first part."

Samira hurriedly stashed the dog beneath the basket

and found a medium-sized rock to put on top of it. The dog leaped around underneath the basket, almost knocking the rock off, but it held.

"It won't be for long, I promise," Samira whispered. She picked up a stick and hurried down the road toward the bridge.

Samira burst into tears—an old trick she was good at by now—a few seconds before the first of the two soldiers saw her and raised his rifle.

"Halt! Who goes there?" he said to her in passable French. And then, when he saw it was a sobbing little girl, he said, "Why are you out past curfew? Where are your parents?"

If she could only tell him where her parents really were—one of them in the ground and the other in a prison, both thanks to soldiers like him. But she kept up the act.

"I've lost my dog," Samira blubbered. "I opened the door just for a moment, and he ran away. Have you seen my dog?"

"No," the soldier said, "and you need to go home right now. It's dangerous to be out after curfew. Go home. Your dog will come back tomorrow."

"No! He'll get lost and never find his way back!"

The second soldier rolled his eyes at the first one. Samira could sense their patience wearing thin. It was time for the dog's part in this little play. All she had to do was call him, and—

—and suddenly Samira realized she had no idea what the dog's name was.

A BIT OF THEATER

Samira needed the dog to come to her rescue—*but what was his name?* She would just have to make one up and hope he still came when she called him. But *what* to call him? Her mind went blank as she struggled to come up with something.

"All right, that's enough now," the first soldier said. He took her arm. She was caught. Trapped. She kept trying to think of a name to call for the dog. All she could see in her mind's eye was the tiny dog, dancing around the fallen soldier, barking bravely as he took on a challenge a thousand times greater than himself. Suddenly, she had it—the name of a similarly brave and talkative character from one of her favorite plays.

"Cyrano!" she called as loudly as she could. "Cyrano! Come! Come on, boy!"

"Let's go," the first soldier said, pulling her away. The second soldier started for a portable two-way radio.

"Cyrano!" Samira cried, her desperation real now. Soon they would be asking to see her papers, and if they discovered they were fake—

There was a thump and a crash from the hedgerows, and a little white dog came tearing up onto the bridge. Samira broke free of the soldier's grasp and went down on one knee to scoop up the little dog—Cyrano now. She hugged him as he licked her face.

"Oh, Cyrano! It's my dog!" she told the soldiers. "I knew he was out here!"

"All right, you've found your dog," the first soldier said. "Time to get you home."

He looked up to say something in German to the other soldier, and Samira quickly tossed the stick far into the darkness beyond the other side. Cyrano leaped from her arms and chased after it.

"Cyrano! Come back!" Samira cried, running to catch him.

"Here, wait!" the German soldier called. "You can't be out after curfew!"

Samira sprinted across the bridge, immediately ducking into the sharp, tangled hedgerow along the side of the road. Twigs and limbs scratched her, but she pushed through, running for all she was worth to put distance between herself and the bridge. As though he had never been gone, Cyrano appeared beside her, yipping as they ran pell-mell through another orchard.

"Not quite the actress I think I am? Ha! Take that, headmistress," Samira muttered.

Chak-chak!

The sound of a handheld machine gun cocking brought Samira up short, and she fell backward into the dirt as a shadowy soldier stepped out from behind a tree.

THE CROSS OF LORRAINE

Samira put her hands up. "Wait! Don't shoot! I was just looking for my dog," she lied.

"Yes, well, you've found something else," said a smooth French voice.

"The *Boches* have given up and gone back to their guard post on the bridge," said another French voice. *Boche* was French slang for Germans. It was from a word that originally meant "cabbage head."

More shadowy figures emerged from the trees all around her, stepping into the moonlight where she could see them. They wore a motley hodgepodge of clothes, from dirty shirts to stolen German military boots to blue overalls. One or two of them wore the torn remnants of British military jackets, probably "borrowed" from pilots who hadn't survived their desperate jumps once their planes were shot down. They all wore white silk scarves cut from parachutes, and each of them carried a weapon of one kind or another—old hunting rifles, stolen German machine guns, British Sten guns dropped into France for the Resistance. One man had a bandolier of bullets slung over his shoulder, and almost all the soldiers had pistols tucked roguishly into the tops of their trousers.

And one of them, the soldier who had first spoken to Samira, wore an armband with the French red, white, and blue tricolor and the double-barred Cross of Lorraine on it—the symbol of Free France, the French government in exile.

Samira hadn't found the Maquis. They had found her.

HIPPOLYTA'S DAUGHTER

"I'm Sa—" Samira began, but the man with the Free France armband cut her off.

"No real names, please," he said quietly.

Right. Of course. Samira remembered—the Maquis all used code names, to protect the others and their own families if they were caught by the Germans. Her mother even had a code name within the organization, since she was a messenger for them.

"I'm Hippolyta's daughter," Samira said, using her mother's code name.

"Yes, I recognize you," said the Maquis leader. "My name is Odysseus." He didn't introduce the others. "Do you have a message for us? Where is your mother?"

Where should Samira begin? With the thing that mattered most to her, she decided.

"My mother's been captured by the Nazis," she said.

The tearful quavering that came into her voice wasn't an act this time, but she tried to put on a brave face. "We were coming to tell you—'The dice are on the carpet. It's hot in Suez.'"

The men stirred excitedly. They all knew what the code words meant—that the invasion of France was happening, at long last. They clapped each other on the back and hugged, then happily got busy loading themselves up with the gear they had hidden away nearby.

Their leader was all business though.

"Your mother, she knew this, and she was captured by the Nazis?" Odysseus asked.

"Yes. But she wasn't captured because she was delivering the message," Samira explained. "She was captured trying to help a family escape one of the Nazi roundups. Retribution for the assassination of Major Vogel, we think."

The happy mood of a moment ago was dispelled at the mention of retribution. They all knew what that meant to the French people. How many people would be murdered.

"They'll have taken her to Bayeux," one of the men said. "That's where they take all the prisoners around here."

"But they don't know that she knows about us," Odysseus said. "They won't even know to interrogate her."

"You still have to help me get her out!" Samira said.

"Get her out?" said a man with a southern French accent. "Impossible. The Bayeux garrison has at least forty soldiers in it."

"But you have to!" Samira begged. "She'll be shot in the morning!"

"Not if the English and the Americans do their jobs," Odysseus said. "If what you heard on the radio is true, the Germans will have far more to worry about in a few hours."

"But . . . what if the invasion fails?" Samira cried.

"It's our job to make sure the invasion doesn't fail," Odysseus said. One of his lieutenants nodded that they were ready to go. Samira couldn't believe what was happening. They weren't going to help her get her mother back!

"*Please,*" she begged.

Odysseus shook his head. "I'm sorry. Even if we wanted to, we couldn't defeat an entire garrison of German soldiers. And those code words you brought to us, they mean more than just the beginning of the invasion. They are specific instructions to us. We are to enact Operation Tortoise and Operation Green: stop the Germans' trains and slow down their trucks so they can't respond to the invasion with full force. I'm afraid that's the only thing we can do to help your mother and the others survive."

They were already leaving. The Maquis were Samira's last, best, and *only* chance to free her mother, and they were walking away. She choked back a sob.

"Then I'm coming with you," Samira said.

THE SWITCHING STATION

"I don't want the girl here," said the Maquis with the southern French accent. "Send her home."

Now that they were moving, sticking to the shadows again, all the Resistance fighters looked like big black shapes against the gray night. Samira followed on their heels, and Cyrano followed on hers.

"I'm not some useless kid," Samira argued. "I can hold my own."

"You should have heard her lay it on for those two *Boches* on the bridge, Perseus," one of the others said.

"No. Not because she's a child," the southerner code-named Perseus said. "Because she's Algerian. She doesn't care about France. None of them do. Just Algeria."

"I've never *been* to Algeria," Samira told him. "I was born and raised in Paris. But either way, we've got a better chance of getting our independence from France, not Germany."

"See?" Perseus said. "It's always Algeria first."

"Sounds like the kid is saying get rid of the Nazis first," the other Maquis replied.

"I don't trust her, is all," Perseus said.

Samira felt her face flush hot at the insult, but all that mattered was that they did whatever they could to help the invasion succeed. Every second the Nazis were distracted, that was another second her mother and the others survived.

"I'm Jason," the friendly Maquis told her. "Of the Argonauts. That's not my real name. If you're coming along, we're going to need a code name for you too. I don't remember Hippolyta having any daughters in her story. How about Atalanta? She was a hunter. Good one too."

"I like Atalanta," Samira said. "You know a lot about Greek heroes. Were you a teacher?"

"Oh, I couldn't say," said Jason. "Not supposed to share too much personal information, you know. But we're quite a troop here. Shopkeepers and soldiers, gutter-snipes and the well-to-do. All *former* shopkeepers, soldiers, guttersnipes, and well-to-do, that is. Now we are all Maquis, and Maquis is all we are."

The little dog sniffed at a hole in the ground.

"That's Cyrano," Samira said. "That's not his real name either."

"Enough chatter," Odysseus whispered back at them. "We're getting close."

It still took them a long time to get where they were going—a stretch of train track that ran along the steep embankment of a rock-filled river. Samira and the others walked parallel to the line for another couple of kilometers until they came to a small railway building beside the tracks. Right outside the house, the single line split into two before both sets of tracks disappeared beyond a bend. It was a little single-story switching station. Inside, an electric light illuminated a tiny room and a single old man sitting by a woodstove reading a book.

"We'll have to kill the old man," one of the Maquis said.

"We can't kill him," said Perseus. "He's French. He's just doing his job."

"Doing his job for the *Germans*," said another.

Samira knew that there were some French people who worked for the Germans because they had to. Others did it because they liked the Nazis and what they stood for, and wanted to be a part of it. Or at least thought they could profit from it. The Maquis hated willing collaborators even more than they hated the Germans. Samira hated them too. Collaborators were French who had betrayed their own.

"If we let him live and he's a collaborator, he could report us as we pass," said another Maquis.

"Why can't you just blow up the train tracks farther back?" Samira asked.

"There's a tunnel up around the bend," Jason explained to her. "We want to do it there. Repairing tracks and clearing a train wreck from a tunnel takes much more time than outside a tunnel. They call it 'Operation Tortoise' for a reason."

Slow down the German counterattack. That was the plan. But would it be enough to save the life of Samira's mother?

"Let's just kill him," one of the shadows argued. "We're wasting time."

"It looks like someone has decided for us," Jason said with a smile in his voice.

Samira looked, and her eyes went wide.

Cyrano was trotting right up to the station's front door.

CYRANO INTRODUCES HIMSELF

"Cyrano! No!" Samira cried. She burst from the bushes where she and the Maquis were hiding and tried to catch the little dog, but she was too late. Cyrano barked, and a pudgy gray-haired man with a short gray beard opened the door. Samira froze. The old man wore brown pants and a blue jacket, with a red kerchief tied around his neck. In his left hand he held a cup of something that steamed.

Samira was perfectly visible to him in the moonlight.

"Well, well, well," the old man said with a smile. He looked first at Samira, then at Cyrano, who trotted inside and turned around three times before settling himself by the woodstove. "Ah," the old man said to Cyrano. "Make yourself at home."

When he turned around again, Odysseus and the

other Maquis had stepped out of the darkness with their guns.

"And who do we have here? Maquis?" the old man said. He put the tips of his fingers to an imaginary hat. "Brigadier Rene de Compiegne, French army," he said smartly, then added, "The last war, of course."

"He's one of the Hairy Ones," said Jason. "Hairy Ones" was a nickname for the French soldiers who had fought in the trenches of the First World War. They often had beards or mustaches, and the nickname stuck.

"You'll be here to blow up the train tracks in the tunnel, then," de Compiegne said. "It's just up around the bend. I'll show you where the telephone lines are too so you can cut those."

Samira could tell the Maquis were surprised. They shared suspicious glances.

"You sound like you were waiting for us," Odysseus said.

"Well, not you personally, but someone from the Maquis. This is an important line. I myself have slowed down German trains on a number of occasions," the old man said proudly. "You'd be surprised how difficult it is to get these old switches to work in a timely manner." He winked, and Samira understood that the "difficulty" with the switches was entirely engineered by de Compiegne.

"None of you know a young Maquis by the name of Elise de Compiegne, do you?" the old man asked hopefully. "She's my daughter. The *Boches* called her up to the Compulsory Work Service last year, and she ran away to join the Maquis rather than be a German slave."

"We use code names," Odysseus said. "I'm sorry."

De Compiegne nodded. "Of course. Of course. That makes sense."

"I think we can trust this one," Jason told Odysseus.

Odysseus agreed, and Samira sighed with relief. She didn't want to see the old man killed just because he was in the right place at the wrong time.

"Atalanta, you stay with the station keeper," Odysseus said.

Samira started to argue, but Odysseus cut her off.

"We're dynamiting a tunnel. It's dangerous work, and I won't have you there. Besides, we need someone to stay here to cut the telephone wires. We'll leave them open until it's done, so as not to arouse suspicion should the Germans try to call."

"There's a phone junction box at the other end of the tunnel," de Compiegne told them. "You can call us from there to tell us it's done."

"Oh, you'll know," Jason said. "Enjoy the warm fire, Atalanta. We'll be back before you can say *boom*."

"Come inside, my dear," de Compiegne said to Samira, heading in. "Do you drink coffee?"

Jason held Samira back. "Keep an eye on him," he whispered, startling her. Hadn't Jason just said the old man could be trusted? And what was she supposed to do if he was a collaborator after all?

There was no time to ask any more questions. Jason and the Maquis were already gone, walking down the track toward the tunnel. Samira followed the old man inside.

Cyrano's eyes peeked open to watch Samira as she sat at the station's little table, then he went back to sleep with a contented sigh. The little dog had clearly already decided the old man wasn't a threat, but now Samira was suspicious.

De Compiegne put a new pot of water on the woodstove.

"This war," he said. "I thought when the first one ended, there would be no more war in my lifetime. Maybe ever again. How could anyone who saw what happened in the First World War ever let it happen again? But here we are."

The long night was catching up to Samira. It was warm and cozy in the little station house, and she could feel herself getting drowsy. She rubbed her eyes to try to wake herself up.

"I hope your daughter is all right," she said.

"Thank you," de Compiegne said. "Is one of those men your father?"

"No," Samira told him. "My father is dead. Killed by the Nazis in Paris. They captured my mother earlier tonight." The pain of seeing her mother dragged away came back to her all over again, and tears welled in her eyes. She put her head down on her arms on the table and looked away so de Compiegne wouldn't see her cry.

"I'm sorry," the old man said. "I do not know if my daughter is alive or dead, so my wife and grandson are all I have left. But perhaps this war will end soon, and we will both be reunited with what is left of our families."

THOOM. The room shook, rattling metal cups and tools, and Samira jerked awake. She had fallen asleep. She was supposed to keep an eye on the old man, and she had fallen asleep!

"I think that was your friends," de Compiegne said. He sat in a chair in the corner, a cup of coffee on a small table beside him and an open book in his lap. Over by the woodstove, Cyrano was awake and alert.

The phone rang, and the old man got up to answer it. Samira rubbed the sleep from her eyes and realized the old man had put a blanket over her. It slipped to the floor. How long had she dozed? Had de Compiegne phoned the German authorities while she had been sleeping? Were Odysseus and Jason and the others about to be rounded up and tortured by the Nazis for information about the Allied invasion? How could she have fallen asleep so fast?

"I see," de Compiegne said into the phone. His voice became urgent. "Yes, of course. I understand. I'll do what I can!" He hung up and turned to Samira. "Quickly, my dear! We must hurry." He snatched up a long metal tool shaped like a T. "Your friends were able to blow the tracks, but not before an unscheduled train got past them—a train loaded down with German tanks!"

SABOTAGE

Samira hurried outside with the station keeper.

"A train with tanks on it got past?"

The tracks were blown—nothing else could get through the tunnel, not until long after the invasion was over. But a train full of tanks could be used against the English and the Americans *right now*, and if the invasion failed—

"But what can we do?" Samira asked.

"See that big lever? The one that switches the tracks?" said de Compiegne. "Move it to the middle, and we'll hammer wooden blocks in the gaps. That might derail the train. In case it doesn't, I'll loosen some of the bolts on the track down the line. We have to hurry though—the train will be on top of us in no time!"

"I'll start loosening the bolts," a familiar voice said. "You two jam the switch."

Samira jumped as Jason emerged from the shadows of the station.

"You!" Samira said. "I thought you'd gone on ahead with the others!"

"Odysseus left me to watch de Compiegne, just in case."

"I thought you said we could trust him!"

Jason shrugged. "I guess I was right. But at least I didn't fall asleep," he said with a smile.

Samira scowled and ran to help de Compiegne with the switch.

"Fetch me a couple of blocks of wood from the woodpile," de Compiegne told her. She was back in seconds, and Cyrano barked happily at her heels. It was all great fun to him, but in minutes a train weighed down with dozens of tanks was going to come barreling by unless they could stop it.

Samira and de Compiegne wedged the blocks in place, and he hammered them home with a sledgehammer.

"Good. Here, quickly," he said, panting. He grabbed another of the T-shaped tools. They ran to where Jason was already working. Each piece of railroad track was about twelve meters long and attached to the big wooden railroad ties by bolts that screwed down to hold it tight. De Compiegne fitted the T-shaped tool over one of the bolts and grunted, trying to turn it. Getting the bolts loose was hard—it took a lot of strength to get them to budge. Jason had only gotten three loose already.

Working together, Samira and de Compiegne were as strong as Jason, and now they were pulling twice the number of bolts loose. "How is taking just one piece of track out going to do anything?" Samira asked as they strained against another bolt.

"All it takes for a thing that big and heavy and fast to come crashing down is to get it to slip its track," Jason explained. "This works better than dynamite, but in daylight the engineers usually see the missing track and stop the train."

Samira felt a shuddering vibration deep down in her stomach. De Compiegne stopped pulling on the T wrench and put his ear to the tracks.

"It's almost here! Quickly! We must get away!" he said.

But they had only taken out half the rail's bolts!

"Quick, hand me that sledgehammer!" Jason cried.

The train was coming around the bend. Samira could hear the steady *chug-chug-chug* of its steam engine. Its headlight illuminated the curve of track. De Compiegne dragged her away as Jason hefted the sledgehammer and brought it down on the side of the rail—*CLANG!*—and again—*CLANG!*—knocking it a few more centimeters askew each time. He kept swinging even as the train bore down on him.

"Jason!" Samira yelled.

Beside her, de Compiegne was frantically waving his arms to one side. He was warning the train they had sabotaged the tracks!

Samira grabbed at his hands and tried to stop him. "What are you doing? Don't tell them what we've done!"

"They can't stop that train in time now, even if they wanted to. Not with how fast they're going," de Compiegne told her. "But those engineers, they're French! We have to tell them to jump!"

Samira understood, and they both jumped up and down, waving their arms to get the attention of the engineers. The train charged closer. Jason still clanged away desperately, fully lit by the train's light now. The engineers saw him and Samira and de Compiegne, and they jumped out of both sides of the engine, tumbling hard and dragging themselves away as best they could. The train plowed through the wooden blocks she and de Compiegne had hammered in at the switch like they weren't there, shattering them like toothpicks as it roared on. Suddenly, Samira was lifted up into de Compiegne's arms, and he ran away from the tracks, Cyrano at his heels.

"Jason! Jason, get out of there!" Samira cried.

She saw Jason leap away at the last second, and then the train hit the empty space where the bent track had once been.

A DIFFERENT STORY

At first Samira thought the train might just fly on past the gap in its rail. Its engine kept chugging, and its wheels kept turning. But then it slumped. Ever so slightly, but it slumped. The engine slipped off its tracks to the right, and then the two-hundred-tonne behemoth went charging down the embankment toward the river, pulling train car after train car of tanks down with it. The engine smashed into the riverbed with a thundering *KROOM*, and then everything went topsy-turvy. With nowhere to go, the speeding train cars rammed into the ones in front of them and flipped, twisted, and went flying, throwing tanks into the air like catapults. *CLANG! KRANG! SPRANG! THOOM!* It was like the world was coming to an end.

Samira and de Compiegne ducked and covered their ears. A loose tank went spinning end over end right toward them, and Samira pulled Cyrano into a hug as the thing bounced and flipped right over their heads. The train cars kept coming and coming for what seemed like forever, screeching and smashing into each other and jackknifing and splashing down into the river below.

And then it was over. The engine's boiler still hissed, and metal still popped and shifted and settled, but there was no explosion, no fire. Just a giant grave-yard of scrap metal and shattered wood surrounded by ruptured earth. Samira couldn't imagine anyone ever cleaning it all up.

Or surviving it.

"Jason!" she cried. She started to run toward the broken train cars and smashed tanks, but de Compiegne caught her and held her back. "But Jason, he's out there somewhere!" she protested.

Rene de Compiegne just shook his head no.

Samira's heart broke. She sobbed real tears for Jason—a man she'd met just an hour ago, and whose real name she didn't even know. But he'd believed in her when no one else would, and he'd given his life to save countless more. Including, Samira hoped, her mother's. But still it wasn't fair, that any one man should have to sacrifice so much.

De Compiegne hugged her tight until she stopped crying, and she wiped her eyes.

"I suppose that's it for me too," de Compiegne said. "The Nazis will figure me for a Maquis collaborator and blame me for this. Which of course is true."

"You can go on the run! Join the Maquis!" Samira told him.

De Compiegne chuckled. "Hiding out in the woods and fighting the Nazis is a young man's game, my dear. I'm too old for it. No, they'll find me here or at home, and they'll be able to read the story of what happened as easily as I read a book."

"*A story,*" Samira said. "Come on. I have an idea."

Samira led the old man back to his station house, which was miraculously still standing. An upended train car lay across its front path.

Inside, Samira tipped over chairs, swept tools off shelves, and tossed de Compiegne's book on the floor.

"What are you doing?" he asked.

"You said the Nazis would read you like a book. So all we have to do is tell them a different story. You were reading a book by the fire. Maquis saboteurs broke in. Smashed the place up. Cut the phone lines."

"Over here," de Compiegne said. He flipped open a metal box on the wall. It was full of black wires. Samira took a pair of cutters from the floor and snipped the phone lines. She tossed them back on the floor when she was finished and pulled a length of rope from the wall. "Then they tied you up!"

"What could I do?" de Compiegne said, playing along. "I am an old man. I didn't want them to wreck the train, but they overpowered me."

Samira smiled. As de Compiegne lay down on the floor, Cyrano licked his face, and Samira tied the old man's arms and legs tight. But not too tight.

"Hey, who else can say they took out a whole panzer division single-handedly, hmm?" de Compiegne said with a smile.

"Will you be all right?" she asked, suddenly worried about leaving him here all night.

"Yes," de Compiegne said. "Someone will want to know where their tanks are, and they will find me soon enough. Thank you, Samira. I hope you are reunited with your mother soon."

"And you with your daughter," Samira said.

Outside the station keeper's house, Samira wondered what to do now. Her mother had told her to get somewhere safe.

But no. Samira would go to Bayeux. That's where her mother was, and her mother was the only person she had left.

In the weird stillness and quiet of the train wreck, Samira heard the drone of airplanes high overhead. She looked up. Mushrooms sprouted in the sky, black against the gray clouds.

Parachutes, Samira realized. The Americans and

English, coming to save them. Coming to save her mother.

"Let's go, Cyrano," Samira told her little friend. "We've done our part here. It's all up to the soldiers now."

OPERATION TONGA

JUNE 6, 1944

THREE HOURS BEFORE THE BEACH INVASION

IN THE SKY OVER THE ENGLISH CHANNEL

ABSOLUTELY AVERAGE

What the hell am I doing here? Lance Corporal James McKay of the 1st Canadian Parachute Battalion wondered. He closed his eyes and held on to his seat for dear life.

Poom-poom-poom-poom.

German anti-aircraft shells exploded in the sky around him. The twin-engine Albemarle troop transport aircraft that James rode in jumped and rocked. *Germany's welcome committee*, James thought. They must be over the Channel Islands. They would be over France soon, and then he and the rest of the soldiers in the plane would parachute down into enemy territory. They would be the first Canadians on the ground in the invasion—some of the first Allied troops from *anywhere* on the ground at Normandy.

The top army brass told them it was an honor. James thought it was a death sentence.

James was nineteen years old, and like many of the other young men in his company, he was going into battle for the first time. James had short brown hair, brown eyes, and one of those unremarkable faces no one could remember. He was average height and average build. Whenever he was told to line up alphabetically, his last name—McKay—put him right in the middle. In high school, before he'd quit to join the army, James had solid Cs across the board in all his classes. Even his hometown, Winnipeg, Manitoba, was at the longitudinal center of Canada. James was absolutely average. He had never done a single thing in his life to stand out, good or bad.

So what am I doing parachuting into France on D-Day? James thought.

"You volunteered for this," Lance Corporal Samuel Tremblay said, as if reading James's mind. James sat facing Sam across the airplane's lone aisle. Sam was a Cree Indian from Quebec. He was thickset, with tan skin, straight black hair, and high cheekbones. Nobody forgot meeting Sam. He was definitely *not* average.

Like James, Sam wore a green-and-brown camouflage jacket, olive-green pants tucked into tan socks, and a green helmet covered with little shreds of fabric meant to help him blend in with the foliage when they landed. James and Sam had been friends since their first training days in England. Now, months later, they were finally crossing the English Channel in a British plane bound for France, wedged in tight beside the other Canadian paratroopers in their platoon.

"Okay, yes, I volunteered for the army," James told Sam. "I had *reasons*. But it was false advertising! They said I'd be defending *Canada*, okay? I thought that meant . . . I don't know, watching the Canadian coast for German U-boats," he explained. "Guarding street corners in Toronto. Patrolling the Northwest Territories on moose-back. Not invading France! How is invading France defending Canada?"

"The best defense is a good offense," said Sam.

"Okay, what does that even mean?" James complained. He shook his head. "I just want to get this over and get back to Canada as soon as possible."

"Why'd *you* join, Chief?" one of the newer recruits asked Sam.

Sam turned to the newcomer. "The Canadian army doesn't use the rank of 'chief,'" he said, straight-faced. "I'm a lance corporal, like Lance Corporal McKay here."

"No, that's—that's not what I meant—" the soldier stammered.

"Then what did you mean, Private?" Sam asked.

"Uh, nothing. Lance Corporal."

Frightened as he was, James couldn't help but smile. Ever since Sam had made lance corporal, just one rank above private, he'd put dozens of soldiers who'd tried to call him "chief" in their place the same way.

"And that," Sam said across the aisle to James, "is why I joined."

Machine-gun fire hit the Albemarle, and James and the other soldiers flinched instinctively. Not that there was anything you could do to avoid getting shot on a plane. Transport planes delivering paratroopers had to fly low—at about one thousand feet—which put them in the range of German anti-aircraft guns *and* machine guns. The rounds hitting the metal fuselage sounded like trash can lids banging in the alley behind James's apartment building on trash day. *Ka-tunk-ka-tunk-ka-tunk.*

Okay, the Krauts are shooting at me. Honest to God shooting at me! James thought. He closed his eyes and tried to take deep breaths.

"What reasons?" Sam asked.

James opened his eyes. "What?"

"You said you volunteered for reasons. What were they?"

James huffed. "Because the Nazis invaded Winnipeg, okay?"

Sam stared at him. "James, the Nazis never invaded Winnipeg."

"They did too," James said.

"James, Manitoba is in the dead center of Canada," Sam said. "It's fifteen hundred miles from either coast. Don't you think the Nazis would invade . . . I don't know, Montreal or Toronto first?"

James sighed. "It wasn't a *real* invasion, okay? It was *If Day*."

IF DAY

James thought back to that day two years ago. It was February in Winnipeg, a month when the temperature never got above freezing. The snow was already piled up head-high on the sidewalks, and the Red River was a three-mile sheet of ice covered with skaters and ice fishermen every weekend.

It was ten o'clock in the morning on a Thursday, and James should have been in math class. But school was canceled for the rest of the day.

Because today was If Day.

James had just pulled out his coat and shut his locker when a hand pushed him face-first into the metal door. *Ker-slam.*

"Where do you think you're going, McKay?"

James knew who it was without even turning

around, before he ever heard him speak. Marvin Lennox. James's personal bully.

Everybody else forgets who I am, James thought. *So why can't Marvin Lennox forget?*

Marvin gave James a quick punch to the lower back, and James arched in pain. He turned, ready to try to fight back, even though he knew it was a lost cause. Marvin Lennox could beat James up on his own, but standing behind him were Marvin's four stupid buddies too.

Marvin and his gang were a year ahead of James, and they were taller and stronger than he was. They were all on the football team and wore their orange-and-brown football sweaters instead of blazers to school. All of them wore their ties permanently loosened and rolled the cuffs up on their pants to show how cool they were. And like Marvin Lennox, they all had their dark hair slicked straight back on their heads like Humphrey Bogart.

James tried to get free, but Marvin pushed him against the lockers, and his hyena pals laughed.

"Let's break it up here and get downtown for If Day," a teacher said, walking past.

Marvin released James and waited for the teacher to move on before leaning in again menacingly.

"How about this for 'If Day'?" Marvin said. "*If* me

and my boys see you downtown today, McKay, we'll kill you. And there ain't nobody gonna save you."

Marvin and his gang walked away, laughing, and James slumped against his locker. The easy thing to do would be to just go home and hide. But If Day promised to be the most exciting thing to happen in Winnipeg since . . . well, since forever.

James pulled on his coat and ran for the door.

He was just going to have to chance it.

The first sign that anything was different were the radio broadcasts. James heard one as he cut through Eaton's Department Store to stay warm. The place was empty, and all the clerks who had to work were huddled, wide-eyed, around the store's radios.

"Attention, citizens of Winnipeg," said a radio announcer with a German accent. "Your city is now under the control of the Third Reich. Adolf Hitler is your führer now."

James's heart leaped. It was starting! He ran to the revolving doors on the far side of the store and pushed his way out—

—and then pushed his way right back in again when he spotted Marvin Lennox and his gang across the street. He flung himself behind a stand of mannequins in the window where he couldn't be seen, and bumped into Charles Hill, a freshman who wrote for the school paper.

"Oh, hello," Charles said, straightening his glasses. "I was just . . . shopping for clothes."

James glanced up at the mannequins they hid behind—ladies' mannequins wearing long evening dresses.

"Okay, I don't think it's your style, Charles," said James. He peeked out from behind the mannequins, looking for Marvin Lennox.

"Are they gone?" Charles said.

"You hiding out from Marvin Lennox too?" James asked.

"He's not happy about the article I wrote about the football team's loss to Kelvin High. Like I'm the one who fumbled on the ten-yard line."

"Okay, looks like they're gone," James said. "See you, Charles!"

James left the store and ran for the riverfront. An air raid siren suddenly blared, making him flinch, and he watched as planes with German Luftwaffe insignia droned by overhead.

James saw his first Nazis in a city park. There were dozens of them. Hundreds. Some of them wore the all-black uniforms of the SS—the dreaded secret police who made people disappear. More of them wore the gray-green uniforms of rank-and-file German soldiers. There were even tanks!

James joined the crowd of Winnipeggers gathering

to watch. The crowd buzzed with excitement, and James hopped up and down. They were all thrilled because they knew this wasn't a real Nazi invasion. It was If Day.

The Canadian government wanted people to buy Victory Bonds to fund the war effort, and to volunteer to fight. But even though the war in Europe had been raging for almost three years now with no end in sight, Europe was a long way from Canada, and it was hard for many people to understand why they should care. So Winnipeg decided to stage "If Day," an elaborate spectacle designed to show the people what would happen *if*, one day, Nazi Germany invaded and conquered Canada. The planes overhead? Royal Canadian Air Force aircraft painted to look like Nazi planes. The German radio broadcasts? Scripted. The Nazi soldiers? Actors, their uniforms rented from a Hollywood production company. James and everyone else had read all about it in the newspaper for weeks, and now it was finally happening.

The crowd cheered at something, and James climbed up on the cold, slippery base of a lamppost to see. Canadian soldiers had arrived to face the "Nazi" menace! The two sides broke into a choreographed battle, firing blanks at each other and pretending to fight hand to hand. "Medics" ran through the battlefield, dragging the "wounded" to medical tents. Anti-aircraft guns fired big booming blanks at the planes overhead.

This is terrific! James thought. It was better than a war movie.

"McKay!" Marvin Lennox cried.

James tore his eyes away from the show and searched the crowd. There, pushing their way toward him through the spectators, were Marvin Lennox and his boys!

STRONGER TOGETHER

James hopped down from the base of the lamppost and crouched low behind the adults, looking for a place to hide. But hands grabbed him and pulled him back up. It was Helen Wilson, a popular girl in his class.

James blushed. "Oh, hi, Helen, I—"

Helen shushed him and turned him around to face the show. She stood right behind him as Marvin Lennox and his boys ran past, still searching for James.

"Thanks," James said when they were gone.

"I hate those boys," Helen said. "Always treating every girl at school like we're stupid and catcalling us. Making every boy live in fear of them. *Everybody* hates them, but nobody does anything about it."

The crowd *oohed*. The Canadian army had lost the battle. The Nazis had control of Winnipeg.

POOM. A cloud of smoke and dust shot into the air

as the Nazis pretended to destroy the Maryland Bridge. The Nazi soldiers in the park came after the spectators to arrest them, and the crowd scattered. James lost track of both Helen and Marvin in the chaos.

The actors dressed as Nazis spent the rest of the day terrorizing the town. They stole lunches from workers in the Great-West Life insurance building. They boarded city buses and demanded to see everyone's papers. They closed Winnipeg's churches and arrested the priests.

Clank-clank-clank-clank! James watched as a tank—an actual tank!—rolled down Portage Avenue.

James ended up near his father's office building, and he watched in horror as Nazis dragged his father down the steps to a waiting truck with all the other lawyers.

"Dad!" James cried. *"Dad!"*

A German soldier held him back. "He's being taken to the internment camp at Lower Fort Garry. You can pay for his release there."

James knew that this was all an act. That the Nazis were Canadians in costume, and that important Winnipeggers who were "arrested" had to donate money to the war effort or stay in "jail" all day. But it was still shocking to see his father dragged away against his will.

James caught sight of Marvin Lennox and his boys up the avenue, and took a detour. At the public library, he saw Nazi soldiers burning books in a bonfire. (Books the library deemed too worn out to read anymore and had donated to the cause.) Workers replaced the street signs on Main Street with signs reading "Hitlerstrasse"—Hitler Street—and the *Winnipeg Tribune* changed its name to the *Winnipeg Lies-Sheet*. James watched with a chill as the Union Flag over city hall came down and was replaced by the red, white, and black swastika of Nazi Germany.

"It must not happen here!" the mayor cried as he was hauled away. "Buy Victory Bonds! Volunteer! We're stronger together!"

We're stronger together. Something clicked for James, and he hurried back through the streets of Winnipeg. If Day was still happening all around him, but he had a different mission in mind.

Half an hour later, James turned a corner at Union Station and ran headlong into Marvin Lennox. They both staggered back and stood staring at each other before James turned and fled. Marvin and his boys ran after him. James pounded down the sidewalk, praying he didn't slip on a patch of ice. Up and over the train tracks he went, and then down into the Forks, the historic park on the banks of the Red River.

James made it as far as the Forks Market before Marvin caught the collar of his coat and dragged him down to the ground. James fell forward on his hands, scraping both up badly. He couldn't worry about his wounds though. Not yet. Marvin Lennox and his gang surrounded him, and the first kick to his side twisted James up and made him scream.

"Leave him alone, Lummox!" Helen Wilson cried.

Marvin Lennox and his boys froze. Helen stood a few yards away, alongside Charles Hill.

Marvin laughed. "Or what, Helen? You and four-eyes are going to sass me to death?"

"Or we do to you what you've been doing to the rest of us for years," Helen said.

Out from behind bushes and trash cans and snow piles came almost thirty other students from their school. Boys and girls from every clique, every club, every class. Over the last half hour, James had collected them all here in the Forks and brought Marvin and his gang right to them.

"What's this? The Losers' Brigade?" Marvin joked. His boys laughed, but less confidently now.

"Every one of us has been bullied by you and your pack of idiots, Marvin Lennox," Helen said, "and we're here to finally put a stop to it."

Helen advanced on Marvin's gang, and the other students, emboldened by their numbers, stepped forward with her, closing in. Marvin and his friends backed away, until James was surrounded by his allies. Charles and another boy helped James to his feet.

"Fine. You win," Marvin said. "But the next time I see you, McKay, you're dead meat."

"No," said Helen. "If you hurt one of us, jeer at us, so much as *look* at one of us cross-eyed, ever again, *you're* dead meat. And that's a promise."

Marvin laughed and pulled his crew away, trying to make it look like he was done with them, but it felt like a victory for James and his friends. They broke out in smiles, and he could feel the relief pouring through them.

"You think it'll work?" Charles asked. "For good?"

"No," Helen said. "Marvin'll try us. He has to, to save face. So we have to be ready to fight."

"We will," James said. "And we'll win. We're stronger together."

And they were. If Day had taught him that.

Which was why that spring, when he turned seventeen, James had volunteered for the Canadian army.

Ka-tunk-ka-tunk-ka-tunk.

Tracer bullets hit the fuselage of the airplane, bringing James back to the present day. He held his head as the plane spun and dove sickeningly. The soldier next to him threw up, either from the motion or nerves. Or both.

"You not going to tell me what If Day was?" Sam asked from across the aisle.

"Never mind, okay?" James told Sam. "It's a long story."

James twisted to look out the door in the floor, but

all he saw was a dense white fog. If *he* couldn't see any-thing, how could the pilot see all the other forty-nine transport planes flying in formation with them? And how would any of them know where their target was in all these clouds?

"I think I can see my house from here," Sam joked, peeking through the hole.

A red light clicked on above them. That meant they were four minutes from the drop zone. James's heart thumped in his chest. This was it. Whether he wanted to be here or not, there was no going back. Rumor had it that the officer at the back of the plane went last so he could shoot any man who refused to jump. The only reason you didn't go through the hole in the floor was because you were already dead.

"Stand up and hook up!" the dispatcher yelled.

It was time to jump.

GREEN LIGHT

James struggled to his feet. In addition to the standard equipment he carried—his Bren light machine gun, extra bullet clips, Webley Revolver, flares, knife, toggle rope, medical kit, canteen, and food rations—James was also carrying a weapon called a PIAT. PIAT stood for "Projector, Infantry, Anti-Tank." The PIAT could fire a bomb that would take out a tank if you got close enough. *Very* close.

James carried the PIAT and six of the two-and-a-half-pound bombs in a separate canvas bag that would dangle from his leg during his descent. Worried he'd come down without something he needed, James had packed far more gear than he had ever practiced jumping with. Altogether he had to be carrying around a hundred pounds of weight. Sam was carrying even more, and James had to help him stand up.

James clipped his static line to the overhead cable that ran the length of the plane. After they jumped, the lines they clipped to the cable would pull tight, yanking their parachutes open for them.

James sucked in a big breath, swaying and bumping into the soldiers on either side of him. He'd thought being chased by Marvin Lennox and his gang was scary. That was *nothing* compared to what he was feeling now. He and the others had practiced jumping over and over again in England, but they had never jumped into a hail of bullets over enemy territory before.

Pa-tunk! A bullet tore through the bottom of the plane. It hit a soldier who was standing near James—in the butt. He screamed and fell, but a medic was there a moment later to bandage him up and get him back on his feet.

Either you were dead, or you jumped.

James's captain stood at the front to address the platoon. "Alpha Company's mission," he began in a loud voice, "is to protect the 9th Battalion's left flank during their attack on the Merville Battery, then cover their advance to Le Plein."

James and all the rest of them had seen the reconnaissance maps. The Merville Battery was a heavily defended, steel-reinforced concrete bunker on the Normandy coast, which housed four 100-mm howitzer cannons that were aimed right at the spot where soldiers would land on the beaches. Le Plein was a small village nearby.

"We will then seize and hold the Le Mesnil cross-roads," the captain continued.

Sure we will, James thought. He had a bad feeling about all of this.

"Once you're down, head toward the objective as fast as you can," the captain told them. "It'll be dark, so fight the enemy at close quarters with knives and pistols and save the rifles for daylight, when you can see who you're shooting at. Take no prisoners. They'll just slow you down."

Through the open hatch in the floor of the plane, James saw that the fog was gone. It had been replaced by white-and-red flak and tracer fire that crisscrossed in the black night sky. They would be lucky if any of them hit the ground alive.

What the hell am I doing here? James wondered yet again. He turned to look at Sam.

"You volunteered for this," Sam reminded him again.

Click! The red light changed to green. But the airplane hadn't slowed down. James frowned. The airplane always slowed down before they jumped in practice.

"Go! Go! Go!" the captain yelled.

James shuffled along in line with the others, cradling his leg pack and the bag with his Bren machine gun in it. There were three men in front of him, then two, then one, and then it was his turn, and James got down on the floor, dangled his legs over the side, and dropped out into nothing.

KNEES IN THE BREEZE

James dropped.

He let go of the bags he held—both were tied to him—and pulled his legs up, knees together. "Knees in the breeze," as their jump instructors called it. He fell for what seemed like an eternity. Shouldn't his chute have opened already? He panicked, worrying suddenly that he'd forgotten to attach his static line inside the plane. Where was the manual release? Was he going to have to pull it? Then suddenly the cable connecting him to the plane went taut and—

WHOOMP.

James's chute opened, jolting him hard. The rope tying the heavy bag with the PIAT and the anti-tank rounds to his leg tightened and yanked him in the other direction, and James screamed in pain. The parachute pulled one way and the bag pulled the other, each of them trying to pull James apart. He stretched his arms down, trying to reach the rope on his ankle. White-hot stars exploded in his eyes. If he could just pull up the bag. Untie it. Cut it. *Something.* But he couldn't reach it. The rough strands of the rope cut into his skin. James's eyes rolled back in his head, and he felt himself losing consciousness. No. *No.* It was going to pull his foot off! It was going to cut right through his ankle and—

Snap!

The rope broke before his ankle did, and the heavy bag tumbled away into the darkness. Gone were the PIAT and the anti-tank rounds, but James didn't care. All that mattered was the sweet relief of freedom. His ankle still throbbed where the rope had cut into him, but he was still conscious and in one piece.

James's arms and legs shook, and his breath came hard and fast, but his parachute seemed to be working. Tracer fire streaked all around him, blotted out here and there by the black silhouettes of dozens more parachutes. Suddenly—*POOM!*—one of the dark shapes dangling from a parachute exploded, and James gasped. He struggled in his harness, trying to back away, but there was nowhere to go. What could the Germans be firing at them that would make a man explode like that? As the shock wore off, he realized there was no mystery—a German machine gun had hit something explosive the man was carrying. A Gammon bomb maybe. James watched in horror as the flames burned through the parachute's cords and the body plunged to the earth.

Oh, God, thought James suddenly, *was that Sam?* But no—Sam hadn't been carrying a Gammon bomb or anything else that would explode like that if it were hit. James let out a heavy breath. But where was his friend? Was he all right?

Red-hot bullets screamed through the air around James, and he cursed and spun, trying uselessly to dodge them. The tracer fire came in high, missing him entirely, but he felt it rip at his parachute, filling it with holes and snapping some of the cords. The holes made him fall faster, and he twisted and turned, trying to see where he was coming down. He watched as another paratrooper hit the ground with a splash and disappeared. A splash? Was he coming down over a lake? There weren't any lakes on the map!

James pulled on his chute, steering away from the water as best he could. He fell faster. Faster. James's heart was in his throat. Where was he going to land? Everything was black. Was he coming down in a tree? A lake? A field full of land mines? Right on top of a German garrison?

The dark earth loomed up at James, and he closed his eyes and braced for impact.

ROMMEL'S ASPARAGUS

James came down hard and fast, tumbling wildly. He bumped and rolled and cursed before thumping to a stop at the base of a tree, completely bundled up from head to toe in his parachute. He was dizzy. Sore. James's leg burned and his left arm throbbed, and his heart pounded a drumbeat in his chest. He shook his head to try to clear the cobwebs and remembered what he had to do next:

Get free of the parachute. Make sure no one saw you coming down.

James wriggled and turned, trying to get at the buckles and latches that strapped him into his parachute harness, but he was hopelessly tangled. He was going to have to cut his way out. He twisted awkwardly and pulled out his knife.

He had just started to saw his way through the

strings when he heard a rustling sound nearby. He froze. Was it German soldiers? Were they combing the field for him already?

It didn't do any good to sit here listening when he was all wrapped up like a present for them. At the risk of being heard, James hacked away at the parachute cords.

The rustling sound got closer. Closer.

Footsteps. James could make them out clearly now. The strings were cut, but he was still tangled in the chute and couldn't see anything. He stabbed at the silk fabric and tore a long gash through multiple layers at once.

Dark sky! Tracer fire! Spotlights! He was through! James blinked and gasped for air. No German soldier stood over him, but the footsteps were getting closer. It sounded like there were two of them. A patrol!

James ripped a bigger opening for himself and struggled through. He needed his machine gun or his pistol, but one was still in its bag, and the other was taped to him so he wouldn't drop it in the air. The pistol was closer to his hand, and he chopped away at the tape that bound it. The footsteps came up right behind the tree he was leaning against. The pistol was free! James twisted around the tree trunk, fell to his elbows, and aimed—

—right into the eyes of a cow chewing its cud.

James put his head down in the grass. Stupid as it was, that cow had almost for real killed him. It had just about given him a heart attack.

The cow lowed softly and moved away, its four feet—the two pairs of footsteps James had heard—rustling in the grass. The cow wasn't a pair of German soldiers, and the tree James had leaned against wasn't a tree either. He saw that now. It was "Rommel's asparagus."

Rommel's asparagus were big poles with sharpened tops that the German field marshal Erwin Rommel had ordered planted in the ground, meant to gore Allied paratroopers and smash the Allied gliders that tried to land in the fields of Normandy. In aerial photos they looked like asparagus growing out of the ground, which was how they'd gotten their name. James shuddered, thinking about how he'd just missed landing on this one.

James took a deep breath and tried to calm down. His body ached, but he had to get going. Move toward his target. But where *was* he?

"James? That you?"

James jumped and nearly had another heart attack, but he recognized the voice at once—it was Sam! His friend emerged from the shadows, a dark silhouette against the glow from the anti-aircraft guns. James and Sam hugged each other. James had never been so glad to see anyone in his whole life.

"Did you come down okay?" James asked.

"Turned my ankle," said Sam. "But I'll be okay. Lost all my heavy gear though."

"Yeah, me too," James whispered. "Any idea where we are? I thought I saw another jumper hit a lake."

"It's not lakes. The Germans flooded the fields."

James cursed. "What am I *doing* here?" He held up a finger at Sam. "Don't say it."

Sam shrugged.

James collected his things. "Come on," he whispered. "Let's see if we can find somebody else and figure out where we are."

They didn't see any more parachutes or jumpers. At the edge of the field though, they found a sleepy two-story farmhouse. The lights were off and no one moved inside—it was after midnight, after all.

"I don't remember this place from the aerial photographs they showed us," Sam whispered.

"Yeah," James said. "We're supposed to be protecting the 9th Battalion's flank, but where are they? And how are we supposed to know where *we* are?"

"I suppose we could just go knock on their door and ask."

James looked at Sam. "Are you serious? What if there are Germans in there?"

Sam shrugged. "Then we shoot them." He held up his machine gun. "That is kinda what we came for. You got any better ideas?"

James didn't, so they walked over to the farmhouse and knocked on the front door.

THAT WAY

James shared a nervous look with Sam as they waited at the front door of the farmhouse. A light came on upstairs, and James gripped the trigger of his Bren gun.

An upstairs window slid up, and a round-faced boy with brown hair and pale skin stuck his head out.

"Um, hello, we're—" James began, but the boy closed the window as quickly as he had opened it and disappeared.

James turned to Sam. "Do you think he's coming down?"

Sam shrugged. "Maybe we should knock again."

They waited for what seemed like an eternity. James was just about to knock again when the door opened and the boy was there, joined by a blinking old woman James took to be the boy's grandmother. The boy had a wide smile and dark eyes, and he hopped from foot to foot excitedly. His grandmother was much more sedate. She had wrinkled white skin and gray hair. They both wore threadbare nightgowns that were coming apart at the seams.

"Um, hello," James said. "We're Canadians. We're here for the invasion."

The boy turned to his grandmother and spoke, delivering a stream of excited French that James didn't understand. He sagged. *Of* course *these people speak French*, he thought. *We're in France!* How were James and Sam ever going to ask them anything?

James desperately tried to remember some of his high school French.

"*Bonjour . . . je . . . m'appelle—*" James began.

Sam put a hand up to cut him off and spoke to the boy and the old woman in perfect French. The old woman's face lit up, and the boy answered back animatedly.

James blinked. "You speak French?" he asked Sam.

"Of course I speak French," Sam said. "I'm from Quebec."

The old woman said something in French and tried to pull Sam inside.

"What are they saying?" James asked.

"She wants us to come in and have tea," Sam said. "The boy is excited for the invasion and is asking lots of questions about our gear."

Sam politely turned down the woman's invitation and gave the boy his flashlight.

The boy and the old woman spoke back and forth with Sam, who translated for James.

"Henri says they have been expecting the invasion for some time now."

"Henri?" James said.

"That's his name. This is Henri Shatto," Sam said, "and his grandmother is Madam de Compiegne. Henri's grandfather is . . . at work. He's some kind of train station manager. Henri's mother is in the French Resistance, which is why he lives with his grandparents."

"Okay, we don't need their whole life story," said James.

Sam said something in French that was clearly about James, and the old woman laughed.

"What are you telling them? What are you saying? Never mind. Ask them where the Germans are. *Où es Alamon?*" James tried.

The boy frowned, and Sam cleaned up the question in French for him.

"Ah!" Henri said, brightening. He pointed to the east.

"The Germans are that way?" James asked, excited to have finally learned something.

Henri nodded and pointed to the south.

"And that way?" James asked.

Henri nodded, said something else, and pointed west.

"And . . . that way," Sam translated.

Henri nodded, said the same thing again, and pointed north.

"And that way," Sam said again sadly.

The boy and his grandmother smiled and nodded.

James and Sam glanced at each other. They were surrounded by Germans.

"The Merville Battery," James said. "Ask them where that is."

That question caused much back-and-forth between Henri and his grandmother.

"It . . . it sounds like it's a long way off from here," Sam said. "About eleven kilometers to the north."

"Eleven kilometers?" James said. He did the quick math in his head. "They dropped us *seven miles* from where we're supposed to be! It'll take us hours to get there—*if* we don't run into any Germans!"

A CHANGE OF PLANS

James and Sam weren't jogging, but they weren't walking either. They found a pace somewhere in between. They had a lot of ground to cover, and they were already late to the party, but they were both wary of running into German soldiers on the way. They had to stay on their guard.

"Henri told me his father was taken away by the Nazis," Sam whispered. "To work as slave labor in Germany. His mother ran away before they could do the same to her."

"You got all that in the five minutes we talked to them?" James whispered back.

"The de Compiegne-Shattos are very nice people caught in a very difficult situation," Sam said.

"Yeah, I know the feeling," said James.

They trotted in silence for a few more yards before James said, "I know why I'm here, Sam—"

"You volunteered."

"Yeah, but you did too. Why? Why are you here?"

"I told you on the plane."

"I thought you were joking."

"James, I'm Cree," Sam said. "I can't even *vote* in Canada. Not if I want to keep my tribal status. In the army I get to still be Cree and have respect. The question *you* need to answer is, why are you *really* here?"

James sighed. "Because I'm an idiot."

A human whistle cut through their conversation, and both soldiers instinctively dropped face-first to the ground, their Bren guns thrust out in front of them. James held his breath and opened his senses, trying to see and hear as far as he could in the night. Sam was just as silent beside him. James's heart thundered in his chest.

Someone in the darkness whispered a Canadian code word, and James relaxed. Sam gave the coded reply, and three shadows rose from hiding a few yards away. They were all privates from the 1st Canadian Parachute Battalion. Two of them were white, and one of them was black. That was something new—the Canadian army had been segregated in the last war, but it wasn't now. James had seen a number of black soldiers at basic training in England.

The two groups briefly introduced themselves. One of the new guys was from British Columbia, and the other two were from back east—Ottawa and Hamilton. The black soldier's uniform was drenched, like he'd landed in one of the flooded fields, and one of the white soldiers had his right arm wrapped up with a bandage. The other white soldier had lots of little cuts all over his face and hands, like his parachute had dragged him kicking and screaming through one of the hedgerows that lined the fields and roads of Normandy.

Two of them were privates from B Company, and one was a private from C Company. James and Sam were from A Company. Only the C Company soldier was in the right drop zone, and all of them were well away from where they needed to be. All their missions were to the north, so they decided to stay together until they could each rejoin their companies.

They had just set off when James heard a sound unlike any other he'd ever heard in real life before. It was like the sound a falling piano made in a cartoon, and it was getting closer, and closer, and—

P-POOM!

A bomb exploded just a few dozen yards away, knocking them all down and showering them with rocks and dirt.

P-POOM! P-POOM! P-POOM-P-POOM!

The bombs fell like rain, and kept falling. The

soldiers scrambled for cover, but there wasn't much of anywhere to hide. James and Sam dragged themselves to the base of one of the hedgerows. Bombs pounded the field all around them. James felt the vibration of each blast in the pit of his stomach and the bottom of his teeth.

"The Krauts found us!" James screamed.

Sam shook his head and pointed at the sky, where the familiar shadows of British Lancaster bombers flew overhead. James watched in horror as they dropped their entire payloads of bombs right on top of them. He couldn't believe it. Their own allies were dropping bombs on them! They were supposed to be hitting German strongholds the ground troops *weren't* attacking. This was a registered paratrooper drop zone!

"They must have gone off course in all the clouds," Sam said.

"Or they chickened out and they're dropping their bombs early so they can get out of here!" James yelled back.

P-POOM-P-POOM-P-POOM-P-POOM!

The bombing went on for more minutes than James could count, and then, as suddenly as it had begun, it was over. The heavy pounding stopped, but the explosions still rang in his ears.

"Our own planes!" the white soldier from British

Columbia yelled. *"Our own damn planes were trying to kill us!"*

"First they drop us in the wrong place, then they bomb us!" James howled.

The white soldier from C Company still lay on the ground, and at first they worried he was dead. But he wasn't injured at all. He was just crying, and he wouldn't get up for a long time afterward. They were all rattled by the bombing. The black soldier walked aimlessly around the cratered clearing just to do something with his shaking body.

"What are we doing here, Sam?" James asked again. "Seriously, what?"

Sam was so unnerved by the bombing he didn't even give James a funny answer. He must have been asking himself the same thing.

"I hope Henri and his grandmother weren't hit," Sam said quietly. James hoped so too.

"Come on," said James. "Let's just get this nightmare over with."

They gathered their wits about them and set off to the north again. James glanced at the sky, wondering if and when their own allies would bomb them again, and he caught the others doing it too.

About thirty minutes had passed when they ran into another fifteen Canadian paratroopers, led by Major

MacLeod from C Company. MacLeod was a tall, thin Nova Scotian with a brown mustache that looked like a horsehair brush. He wasn't from James's company, but he was now the ranking officer in the group.

"I was supposed to have a heavily armed force of more than a hundred men, with machine gunners, heavy mortars, Bangalore torpedoes, the lot," MacLeod declared.

He certainly didn't have that now. James counted twenty men with nothing more than three machine guns, eight Bren guns, a few pistols, and one PIAT.

"We'll have to do," said MacLeod. "We have a mission: Destroy the enemy radio station at Varaville, capture or destroy the enemy headquarters there, and blow the bridge over the Divette River." He paused and looked around. "And that's just what we're going to do."

James shot a disbelieving look at Sam. Do all that with just twenty men? The major was nutters.

"But, sir, we're not with Charlie Company," Sam said.

"You boys from other companies are too far away from your objectives to make it in time," MacLeod told them. "We're near Varaville. With your help, we have just enough men to give it a go. Listen," he told the whole group, "we don't fulfill our objectives, and all those boys coming off the boats in a few hours are going to have more fight than they can handle. We're here to do a job, and by God we're going to do it."

And just like that, James and Sam were off to attack the Nazis at Varaville.

GOLDILOCKS AND THE TWO CANADIANS

From where James hid, he could see the German headquarters in Varaville. It was located inside a fancy château on the edge of town. The large house was white with tall windows and a steep slate-gray roof. Three smaller buildings of white-and-gray stone, miniature versions of the château, sat nestled up against its sides, like puppies sleeping around their mother. The house was at the far end of a long, paved driveway lined with trees. Much closer was a yellow-brick gatehouse that would have easily passed for a mansion back in Winnipeg.

Major MacLeod signaled for James and Sam to go into the yellow gatehouse with two other soldiers to check it out. The place was silent as a grave, and when James and Sam came through the front door, Bren guns at the ready, they understood why. The gatehouse was being used as barracks, with every inch of space taken up by bunk beds. Every single one of the beds had recently been slept in but was now empty.

"Somebody's been sleeping in my bed, Papa Bear," Sam said.

"Ninety-six somebodies," James said. There were eight rooms, and six double bunks to a room. And not one Goldilocks in the building.

From a second-floor window, James and Sam could see the German defensive position. The Nazis were set up in a long trench on the other end of the lawn, near the house. The trench was reinforced with dirt and concrete, as was a large bunker that might have been a command post. Machine gun bays stood along the length of the trench. James could even see some of the Germans' round gray helmets moving back and forth through a narrow slit in the front of the bunker. He huffed. Besides almost killing the Canadian paratroopers, the British bombing had evidently awakened the sleeping Germans and put them on the defensive. James and Sam shared a knowing look—a full-frontal assault on the Nazis now would be a suicide mission.

Luckily, Major MacLeod seemed to agree.

"Ninety-six empty beds means ninety-six enemy soldiers," the major said when they told him their news. "That's almost five times more men than we have. We'll have to try to draw them out."

Major MacLeod arranged most of the soldiers as best he could behind a low wall and a shallow ditch near the gatehouse, facing the château. The small Canadian troop was now in a line parallel to the Germans, separated by the long, flat grass lawn.

The major kept a small group that included James and Sam with him at the gatehouse.

"All right. Let's just hope they haven't seen us yet," the major said.

POOM! The wooden gate that blocked the driveway exploded in a blizzard of splinters. No one was killed, but the explosion knocked everyone standing to the ground.

"Good lord, they've got a heavy gun," Major MacLeod said.

And they've seen us, James added silently. That command post he'd seen—the one with the reinforced concrete bunker and the narrow slit in the front—that must be where the big gun lived.

The Nazis in the trench began firing their rifles and machine guns, and the Canadians answered back with what they could from their hiding places. It was a full-on battle now.

"Pass the word for the soldier with the PIAT," the major said. "We'll try to get a bead on the Germans' big gun from the second floor of the gatehouse. You and you"—he nodded at James and Sam—"guard the down-stairs doors."

Major MacLeod hurried upstairs with three other soldiers, including the corporal with the PIAT, while James and Sam took up defensive positions on either side of the first floor. Moments later James heard the distinctive *shunk* of the British anti-tank weapon being fired from a second-floor window, and he took a peek outside.

The PIAT bomb landed with a *BOOM*, kicking up smoke and sod, but it fell too short to do any damage to the German gun or any of the Nazi soldiers in the trench. James cursed, but he knew the corporal with the PIAT would be saying much worse right now as he hurried to reload and try again.

KRAKOOM! The second floor of the gatehouse exploded, buckling the ceiling above James. He ducked and staggered outside, where dust and debris were still settling. Broken glass and pieces of brick crunched under his boots. He looked up. The roof was still on the gatehouse, but the second floor was a smoking hole. The German gun had scored a direct hit on the building. *But the same shell that destroyed the gate isn't nearly power-ful enough to do* that, James thought. Then he realized: The shell must have hit the corporal's extra PIAT rounds. That's what had caused the huge explosion.

The corporal—the major! James hurried back inside, but Sam met him coming out.

Sam shook his head. "Don't, James. They're all dead."

REINFORCEMENTS

Four men killed in a single blast. And with them had gone their only heavy gun.

James put a hand to the wall of the gatehouse and said a silent prayer for the major and the other men. If Day, the practice jumps in England, the anti-aircraft fire over the Channel, parachuting into France, the British bombing—each of them had been real, and frightening, in their ways. But the way Major MacLeod and the others had been there one moment and then just— just *obliterated* the next, chilled James to the bone. The thought that his life might end instantly, explosively, in the fraction of a second, scared a stillness into him he knew would be with him the rest of his life.

Sam put a hand on James's shoulder, and James nodded. James would be all right. He wanted to be anywhere but here in France, anywhere but fighting this war, but there was no way out but forward. No time to *not* be all right.

Together, James and Sam abandoned the gatehouse and joined the other paratroopers shooting from cover. A captain took over for the major, but there wasn't much to do besides snipe at the heads of German soldiers who sniped at the Canadians. Even the German big gun became useless—it was too big to target individuals and too small to destroy the Canadian defensive positions. It was a stalemate.

Sam turned his back to the German defenses and leaned against the low stone wall, out of sight from the snipers.

"So I guess we just settle in until reinforcements come?" Sam asked.

"Yeah—but *whose* reinforcements, ours or theirs?" James asked. They both knew the likely answer to that—there were far more Germans in Normandy right now than Allied soldiers.

"Hey, what's happening, fellows?" someone asked, and James and Sam both jumped.

Two Canadian paratroopers strolled out of the darkness, one with blond hair, the other with red hair. Both were privates. The blond soldier held a Bren gun by the barrel, carrying it backward over his shoulder. The redhead carried a two-inch mortar and at least six mortar bombs that James could see strapped to his web belt.

"Take care of the Krauts already?" the blond soldier asked.

James and Sam grabbed the men by their belts and dragged them forcefully to the ground just as bullets tore through the air where they had been standing. Over the smaller fire they heard the *POOM* of the German big gun, thrown in for good measure. The shell landed far down the road with a *BOOM*, taking out a tree.

James caught his breath. If that big gun had hit the soldier with the mortar shells, the newcomers would have been vaporized—and James and Sam along with them.

"No, we haven't taken care of the Krauts yet," Sam said.

"Yeah, so I see," said the blond private, readjusting his helmet. "We're Bravo Company. We were totally lost, and then we heard the gunfire—that's how we knew where you were. But when it stopped awhile back, we figured the fighting was over."

"Sounds like the Jerries have a 75-mm gun," said the redhead.

"We haven't had anything big enough to take it out," James said. He nodded toward the small metal tube the redhead carried. "Think you can hit it from here with your mortar?"

The private took a peek over the wall and ducked back down just before a German bullet hit the top of the wall, kicking up the kind of mortar that held rock walls together. "Friendly," the private said.

"Yeah, they're regular Betty Boops," said James.

The redheaded soldier shook his head. "A two-inch shell's not gonna do any good against that bunker they've got protecting it. It's just gonna tickle the top of it."

James understood. Mortars worked by lobbing bombs at high arcs toward their targets. Mortars struck from above—which didn't help much if the bunker was covered over with thick concrete. The weakest part of a bunker was the slit in the front that the big gun fired out of.

Which gave James an idea.

"Okay, let me have that mortar and some bombs," James said.

The redheaded private looked confused. "Do you know how to aim a mortar?"

"I don't need to," James said excitedly. He took the mortar and the bombs from the private. "Come on, Sam!"

Sam didn't ask where they were going. He followed along silently as James crawled away from the

Canadian position, staying low in a shallow drainage ditch. The ditch took them to a line of trees on the far side of the château's front yard, where James had a clear line of sight to the gun emplacements. Bullets hadn't followed them, and rifles weren't sniping at them now, so he hoped they hadn't been seen.

Without a word, James prepared the mortar, and Sam unpacked the shells. James watched his friend for a moment, suddenly aware that the shells in Sam's hands were likely to do to some Germans what their big gun had done to Major MacLeod and the others. James hated the thought of anyone dying that way, but this was a war, and he had a job to do.

Mortars were designed to be planted on the ground and then tilted and fired, but James had other plans. He found a small but sturdy-looking tree and held the mortar to it, aiming it almost horizontally at the slit in the German bunker.

Sam smiled and nodded.

To fire a mortar, you dropped a bomb into the tube, and gravity did the rest. The back end of the bomb would strike a pin at the bottom of the mortar's barrel, triggering an explosive charge that launched the mortar back up the tube and toward its target. Without gravity to activate the bomb, Sam was going to have to do it himself.

James held the mortar steady. Sam took the first of

the bombs, slid it partway into the barrel of the mortar, and nodded once, twice—

On the third nod, they both turned their heads away, and Sam shoved the missile hard down the barrel.

POOM! The mortar shell fired almost instantaneously, and a second later the front of the big gun's bunker exploded in a cloud of white dust.

Yes! Success! James almost couldn't believe it had worked. There was no time to rest on his laurels though. James waved at Sam to keep the shells coming, and he aimed for one of the machine-gun emplacements. *POOM. POOM. POOM. POOM.* They got off four more rounds, one for each of the machine guns and one more for the big gun, and then dove for the drainage ditch, expecting return fire.

But nobody fired back.

James heard a cheer go up from the direction of the yellow gatehouse, and he peeked out of the ditch to see a Nazi soldier waving a white flag from one of the bunkers.

The Germans were surrendering.

James stood up in wonder. He and Sam had done something that worked. Something that had saved more of his comrades from being killed. He felt a tingle of—what was that feeling? *Triumph?* The last time he'd felt that way was when he and the other students in Winnipeg had made Marvin Lennox back down. But this victory was so much greater than that one.

James and Sam hurried to join their comrades as a captain accepted the Nazi surrender. There were only forty-three German soldiers uninjured enough to surrender, but they still outnumbered the Canadians almost two to one.

When the German soldiers saw how few Canadians there were, and how many more of them there were, they fumed at one another. James didn't have to understand German to know how angry they were to discover that they had surrendered to an inferior, less-well-armed force.

"Exceptional work, gentlemen," the Canadian captain told James and Sam. "If we get out of this alive, I'm recommending you both for a commendation."

Exceptional, James thought. *The captain called me exceptional. He's going to recommend me for a commendation!*

James was stunned. It was the first time in his life he could remember anybody ever calling him anything but average. Maybe the army was a place where he could be more than he was back home.

But what did that say about him? That he was average and forgettable as a civilian, but as a soldier he was exceptional and commendable? Was that the person he wanted to be?

James knew he should be happy. His gambit had worked. They had beaten the Nazis! Taken the château!

But at what cost? And how did this help Canada? Why *were* they here?

"We counted ninety-six beds," the Canadian captain told the paratroopers. "Unless we managed to kill and injure fifty-one Nazis, there may still be Germans inside the château who haven't surrendered."

He dispatched three teams of two to search the first and second floor of the château, as well as its basement. James and Sam were one of the teams. The captain assigned the first floor and the second floor to the other two teams.

James and Sam were assigned the basement.

I wish I was average and forgettable again, James groused to himself.

WHEN DAY

James stood in the empty kitchen, covering Sam with his Bren gun. Sam flung open the door to the château's basement and jumped back.

Nothing. No shouts, no bullets, no grenades. Just a set of wooden stairs, disappearing down into darkness.

Upstairs, James heard nervous scuffling, then a relieved cry of "All clear!" The first floor had been empty too. If there were any German soldiers in the house, they were in the basement.

"What the hell am I doing here?" James asked for the million and fourth time.

"You're going down there first," Sam said.

"What? You go down there first!"

Sam shook his head. "I'm the senior officer."

"We're both lance corporals!" James protested.

"I made corporal before you did."

"By one week!"

"So I order you to go down first because I'm one week your senior officer," said Sam. "And also I'm afraid of the dark."

"That's low, Sam. Real low."

James sighed. He'd hated going down into the basement of his own house since he was a boy. Still did, truth be told. The creaky stairs, the cobwebs, the dark shadows, the damp chill. Once, his younger brother had locked him in down there as a prank, and he'd sprained his wrist hammering on the door in his panic to be let out. The memory sent a shiver down his back, and he felt a gnawing pinch in his stomach.

The only time he'd ever been that scared again was when Marvin Lennox and his gang had chased him through the streets of Winnipeg on If Day.

And today, of course.

But the other soldiers were waiting for the all clear. Chest heaving, James lifted his Bren gun again and inched toward the door. He peered down, trying to see, but it was too dark. A light switch had been wired to the wall just inside the door, and arm shaking, he slowly shifted his left hand from his gun to flip it.

Nothing. There was no bulb, or no electricity, or both.

James moved on to the landing at the top of the stairs, waiting for his eyes to adjust. He tried to tiptoe down the steps, back pressed to the wall on his right, but the treads were just as old and creaky as his basement stairs back in Winnipeg. They gave him away with every shift in his weight.

Forget sneaking around, James thought. If there was a German waiting to shoot him down there, he couldn't have telegraphed his arrival better if he'd marched down crashing cymbals together.

"Is there anybody down there?" he called. *"Geb auf!"* he added, using what little German he remembered from their training to order whoever was down there to surrender.

James was afraid his quaking legs would go out from under him if he didn't move, and he rushed the rest of the way down the stairs. At the dirt floor he backed into a corner. Cobwebs grabbed at his neck underneath his helmet, making him shudder. The damp, earthy smell of every basement everywhere in the world washed over him, and he felt his old panic rise up within him.

There was a grimy window high up on the opposite wall, and in the brown light he saw movement in the far corner. His heart jumped into his throat, and he thrust his gun at whatever it was.

"Who's there?" he said, his voice squeaking.

A man and a woman came out of the shadows, and James's finger tightened on the trigger. But the man and the woman weren't soldiers. They were small.

Thin. The woman wore a threadbare dress, the man much-patched trousers and shirt.

Behind them, clinging to her mother's skirt, was a dark-haired little girl.

James felt himself start to breathe again, but he was still panting. Still scared.

"Sam! Sam, get down here," James called. "There's French people down here."

Sam hurried down to join him and began speaking to the family in French. The trio's eyes lit up, and the father leaped forward to shake first Sam's hand, then James's hand, clutching at him like he was a man falling off a cliff.

"He's the groundskeeper, and his wife is the cook," Sam translated. "They say there are no more Germans here—the soldiers all went outside to man the defenses."

Before Sam could finish speaking, the woman took James's face in her hands and kissed him on both cheeks, tears rolling down her face. She hugged him tight, and James felt embarrassment creeping up his cheeks. The woman let him go at last and did the same thing all over again to Sam.

James's eyes had begun to adjust to the darkness, and now he saw the three straw mats on the floor, the small table with the nub of an extinguished candle melted down on it, the three empty bowls.

They're not just hiding down here, James realized.

They live down here. They serve the Nazis like slaves while the Germans eat and sleep and live upstairs.

"Let's get them out of here," James said. If he'd been scarred by being locked in the basement once as a kid, he couldn't imagine how this family must feel. They would never want to go near a basement again.

The woman held a hand up and sent the daughter scurrying away after something. She came back a moment later with an old bottle of wine.

"They've been hiding this from the Germans," Sam explained after the woman said something to him in French.

"Tell them we'll drink it upstairs," James said. "Together."

The father kept shaking their hands, and the mother kept giving them kisses, but James and Sam managed to get the family started up the stairs. As they climbed, the little girl slipped her hand into James's hand.

He smiled down at her and squeezed her hand, and in that moment, James understood. France was a country where If Day had come true. All those things they had pretended had happened in Winnipeg—the Nazis invading, the people's rights and property taken from them, people imprisoned and enslaved—those things had actually happened here. Seeing men in Nazi costumes marching down the cobblestone streets of the Old Market had moved James to enlist, but the threat hadn't been *real*. Not to Winnipeg. Not to Canada. He and Sam and all the other soldiers had known that, the same way they knew France had really been invaded by the Nazis. But France was half a world away. Who cared what happened to France, as long as it didn't happen to Canada?

That's what he had thought then. What he had thought just an hour ago, at the gatehouse, when the Nazis had been shooting at him. But Henri Shatto and his missing parents, the Allied planes dropping bombs on everyone in Normandy, friend or foe, this family living like prisoners in the basement of the château—in the space of a few short hours, James had seen what happened when If Day became When Day.

Nobody should have to live like this, under the boot of Nazi rule, anywhere in the world, James thought.

A deep, freeing calm came over James, and suddenly he understood why he was here. He was going to keep fighting the Nazis as hard as he could until all of France was liberated. And then he was going to move on to free Belgium, and the Netherlands, and everywhere else the Nazis had conquered.

He was going to free every last country where If Day had come horribly true.

But he couldn't do it alone. He needed Sam, and the other Canadian soldiers, and the English and American soldiers who were to follow them. Like the kids back in Winnipeg coming together to stand up to Marvin Lennox, it would take all of them to face down Hitler, the biggest bully in the world.

James saw Canadian paratroopers swarming the château when he came back up from the basement. The French family was quickly handed off to the company medic.

"We moving on?" James asked Sam. Now that he knew why he was here, he was eager to get to it.

Another soldier heard James and shook his head. "Radio tower's been destroyed, and captain sent some men to blow up the bridge. So we're supposed to stay and defend this position until the boys come up off the beach."

"*If* the boys come up off the beach," Sam said quietly.

"They have to make it," James said. "We're here for a reason."

OPERATION NEPTUNE

JUNE 6, 1944

6:30 A.M.

OMAHA BEACH

NOWHERE TO GO

What the hell am I doing *here?* Dee thought, panicking.

He was standing in the Higgins boat. The ramp had just splashed down. They had finally landed on Omaha Beach. It was D-Day, and they were invading France, and—

"Go! Go! Go!" Sergeant Taylor cried.

Chung-chung-chung-chung-chung.

Before Dee could even take a step, the German machine guns on the cliffs beyond the beach tore into the boat, mowing down the first rows of soldiers.

Dee ducked as the bullets flew. The soldiers in front of him screamed as they were shot. It was like the Jerries had just been waiting for the ramp to come down!

"Go! Move! Let me out of here!" soldiers yelled.

But where? Dee wanted to know. Into the hail-storm of bullets? To stay in the boat was to die. To push forward was to die. Everything around Dee was suddenly death. Some of the men tried climbing the tall walls of the boat and jumping over the side, but they were shot too.

Sid pushed forward, head down, and Dee followed, his heart thumping in terror. The soldier to his left, a man named DeLuca, was hit and went down, where he was crushed underfoot. Sid was still up and surging forward.

Dee climbed over dead and dying men to get to the edge of the ramp. He expected a bullet to hit him any second now. He wondered, weirdly detached, if he would feel it or whether he would just be dead. His heart in his throat, Dee jumped into the water. He thought it was going to be shallow, but to his surprise he dropped straight into five feet of ocean. The cold and the shock took his breath away, and he swallowed seawater as a wave washed over him. The boat must have hit a sandbar! They had been dropped too far out!

Bullets *fwipped* into the water all around him. One struck Dee in the left arm, sending a shooting pain up through his shoulder and down through his fingertips. Another dead soldier fell into the water beside him. Was it Sid? There was no way to tell. Everything was happening too fast, too fast!

I'm going to die, Dee thought in a blind, thrashing

panic. *I'm going to drown. I'm going to be shot again, and I'm going to die!*

Dee kicked off the sand and came up for a painful, desperate breath before sinking again. He activated the CO_2 cartridge on his life vest, but it wasn't enough to lift him up out of the water. He was still too heavy. He had too much gear. He fought to unclip the ponderous assault vest he wore over his uniform, his movements slowed by the water and made shaky by fear. At last he was able to slip the vest off. He let go of the sling that carried his rifle too. He couldn't worry about whether he'd need it later. If he didn't get lighter, didn't get out of the water, there wasn't going to be a later.

Lungs burning, eyes stinging, Dee kicked again, breaking the surface.

This time he floated, and what he saw as the waves took him up and down was a scene from hell.

Dead bodies bumped into Dee, and the sea was dark with blood. Men screamed and cried out for medics who weren't there. German pillboxes on the high cliffs laid down a deadly cross fire. "Czech hedgehogs"—huge three-legged, three-armed anti-tank obstacles made from steel bars welded together into an X shape— littered the beach, undamaged by the Allied battleship barrage. Soldiers lay crumpled on the wet sand around the obstacles like stones.

Behind him there was a loud *BOOM*, and Dee turned to see one of the Higgins boats explode in a ball of black smoke and orange flame, hit by a German artillery gun.

"Help! Help, I can't swim!" someone yelled nearby. It was Sergeant Taylor.

Dee *could* swim, and he instinctively went toward the voice, even though they'd been coached to push on up the beach, not hang back to help injured soldiers. That was the job of medics, they were told. But Dee didn't see any medics. Just chaos.

Dee got to Sergeant Taylor and tried to pull him up out of the waves, but the sergeant was too heavy. Dee took a deep breath and dove under the water to unclip and remove the sergeant's assault vest. Once that was done, it was easier to get the sergeant's head above water, and Dee hauled them both toward the beach.

Toward the German guns.

POOM. An underwater mine went off, and a soldier screamed briefly as his body was flung into the air before coming back down with a sickening thunk. *It's not Sid*, Dee thought, realizing he'd lost track of his friend. Where was he? There—Sid was wading through the water, his rifle held high above his head to keep it dry. Sid was alive!

A mortar explosion geysered water behind Dee, and he picked up his pace, dragging the sergeant closer to the beach. Closer. The water got shallower as Dee slogged along. The ocean came up to his chest, then his stomach, then his waist, and then Dee was staggering, walking through the waves, not swimming.

"You can stand up now, Sergeant!" Dee said. But when he turned, he saw that Sergeant Taylor had been shot through the neck while Dee had been pulling him to shore. Sergeant Taylor was gone. Dee had been dragging a dead man.

Dee stood where he was, the waves crashing into him, the bullets and mortars hitting the water all around him, his dead sergeant's jacket still clutched tight in his fist. The sergeant looked up at him, his dead eyes staring through him. Past him. Dee's own eyes lost their focus, and his mind detached from his body, left him standing there senseless in the middle of the havoc all around him. His entire world shrank down to the sergeant's body bumping into him again and again in the blood-dark sea.

Where was he? How had he gotten to this place? What was the point of it all? It was like he was watching a movie of someone else's life, only in color. No, not a movie, a dream. He was standing in the middle of a dream that would be over when he woke up.

"Dee! Pull yourself together!" Sid called.

Dee looked up. His friend was crouched low in the surf a few yards away.

Dee blinked. The beach. The guns. The cliff. The bodies. He saw it all, understood where he was, what he needed to do, but it was too much. He couldn't decide what to do, couldn't move.

"Dee—*Dee!*" Sid cried, running toward him.

And then— *Ssssssss-THOOM!*

A mortar fell between them and exploded.

THE HEDGEHOG

The explosion knocked Dee down and showered him with water and sand and shrapnel.

Dee spluttered in the waves and shook his head as he came back to his senses. There was a crater in the beach between where he was and where Sid had been. But Sid was gone. His friend had been there one second, and gone the next.

"Sid! *Sid!*" Dee cried. Where was he? Had the mortar blown him to pieces? Thrown his body a dozen yards away? Dee couldn't know. But Sid was gone, and all because Dee had lost his head!

Dee cowered in the surf, hopelessly overwhelmed. All around him, more boats were unloading soldiers into the storm of bullets and mortars and mines. More bodies floated in the water. More boats burned, the acrid smell of gasoline and gunpowder and smoke filling his lungs. More men lay screaming on the shore.

This was hell, and Dee had to get out of it.

Water streamed off him as he stood, and Dee charged up the beach through the ankle-deep surf. He looked for Sid as he ran, but he wasn't there, wasn't there. Machine guns on the cliffs belched—*brrrrrrrrppppp-brrrrrrrppppp*—and bullets hit the sand all around Dee with a sound like someone sucking in a breath. *Sif-sif-sif-sif-sif.* Dee felt a warmth in his pants where he'd peed himself, but it didn't matter. Nothing mattered but getting up and off the beach. He was too full of adrenaline, too panicked to stop. If he stopped, he was dead. He had to find cover somewhere. Get out of the open.

Farther ahead, Dee saw soldiers lying dead behind the crest of a dune. No—they were alive! There was a shell line, where the sea swept away from the dry sand at a steep angle, and the soldiers who'd survived that far found that if they lay flat, with their heads pointed toward the cliffs and their feet toward the ocean, they had a tiny bit of cover. The angle was just low enough for the German machine guns not to hit them. But the shell line was too far away from Dee. He couldn't see how he would ever make it without being killed.

One of the big metal hedgehogs was closer, and Dee sloshed over to it and threw himself behind it. Bullets pinged off it a second later—*tink-tink-tink-tink*—and he felt one rip through his jacket but miss his arm. He noticed for the first time that his uniform was shredded and dark red in two other places—low on his right leg and up near his left shoulder. Dee hurriedly wrapped both wounds with bits of cloth to stem the bleeding.

Down the beach, two soldiers waded to shore, then broke for his hedgehog at a run.

"Come on! Hurry!" Dee called, urging them on.

One of the two soldiers plowing through the surf wore a bulky radio unit on his chest, slowing him down.

"You can make it!" Dee called to him.

The two men were close when bullets kicked up sand around them—*sif-sif-sif-sif*—and the radio man went down.

"I'm hit! I'm hit!" he yelled, in obvious pain. "Medic!"

The other soldier kept running, and Dee helped pull him into the shelter of the hedgehog. Dee was just moving to go get the injured radio man when a soldier with a medic's armband—white with a red cross on it— ran over and went to his knees beside him. There were medics on the beach!

Dee's elation was fleeting. A new hail of bullets cut down the medic where he knelt and finished off the radio operator, leaving them both dead in the sand.

Dee gasped and recoiled at the horror of it, the awful cruelty of a Nazi gunner who would shoot a wounded man and an unarmed medic. Dee didn't know when he'd started to cry, or when he would ever stop.

"You have to clear out!" the other soldier hiding behind the hedgehog told him.

Dee blinked at him through his tears. What did the man mean? There was plenty of room here for both of them, and everywhere else around them was death and destruction. Why would they ever leave it?

The soldier held up a Gammon bomb, one of the bulky explosive devices some of them carried. "The hedgehog—the obstacle," he said, pointing to the big steel thing they hid behind. "It has a mine on top! I have to blow it up before the tide comes in! Keep the boats from hitting them later on. It's my job. You have to get out of here."

Dee couldn't believe it. A mortar hit close by, and he flinched. Go back out? Into that nightmare? It had to be thirty yards to the shell line. But the engineer was already standing to attach his bomb. Dee had to find some other shelter, but where? This was madness. What kind of invasion was this? Who had decided they should come ashore in daylight, into the teeth of the German guns? Why hadn't the naval bombardment taken out the pillboxes on the cliffs? Where was their air support? Where were the tanks that were supposed to cover the soldiers' advance up the beach?

This had to be the worst invasion in history.

OPERATION AMIENS

JUNE 6, 1944

MIDMORNING

JUST OFF THE COAST OF NORMANDY

WILLIAM
THE CONQUEROR

This is going to be the greatest invasion in history,
Private Bill Richards thought.

Bill sat on top of his Sherman tank, *Achilles*, watching the explosions on the French beaches through his binoculars. Bill was nineteen years old and built like the tank he drove—squat, wide, and barrel-chested, with close-cropped black hair. He was as bullheaded as a tank too. The son of a Liverpool dockworker, and the youngest of six children, Bill had learned early on to laugh off most slights and hold his own when it came to a fight.

Bill was itching to get into *this* battle, but right now, he and his tank crew weren't getting anywhere.

Their tank was still on their landing craft—a gray, flat-bottomed boat long enough and wide enough to carry three tanks end to end. Their boat was fighting against the current offshore. Some of the other boats in their flotilla had already released their tanks at sea, and Bill swung his binoculars over at them for a closer look. Rigged with screens and propellers that turned them into ersatz boats, the tanks rocked and rolled in the heavy waves as they pushed on toward shore.

"You know what's funny?" Bill told his crewmates while they waited. "Almost nine hundred years ago, William the Conqueror and the Normans left from just about this very place in France"—he nodded toward the shore—"and invaded England. Battle of Hastings and all that. And now we're going back! The English invading Normandy."

"Here we go," moaned Private George Davies, the tank's gunner. Davies, who had a long neck, a Roman nose, and blond hair that swept down to his eyes, was from a wealthy London family and had graduated from an expensive boarding school. Somehow even the grease-covered canvas jumpsuit they all wore looked newly cleaned and pressed on him. "Professor Richards is about to lecture us again."

"I'm named for him, you know. William the Conqueror," Bill went on, ignoring Davies. "William Richards, see? That's why I took an interest. All me brothers and sisters are named for English kings and queens too. Richie, Bess, Vicky, George, and Henry." Bill thought of his siblings back home and smiled.

Davies snorted. "Never have such regal names been assigned to such common stock," he said.

"The only common stock I know of belongs to your father, who's getting rich off government contracts," said Private Thomas Owens-Cook. The son of a member of Parliament, Thomas could out-fancy-talk Davies any day of the week. As Bill's co-driver in the tank, he was the backup in case Bill was injured; as Bill's best friend in the tank, he was ready to back up his buddy in a fight. Not that he would have done much good. Thomas was barely eighteen and hadn't filled in his tall, gangly frame. His Adam's apple stuck out like the knob on a tree, his brown hair was permanently in need of a comb, and he was incredibly clumsy. Still, his heart was in the right place. And he had given up a scholarship to Oxford University to enlist in the army, which Bill esteemed highly.

Private Bryan Murphy, the tank's redheaded gun loader, leaned over the rail and smoked a cigarette, staying out of their squabbling. In two years of service, Bill had heard the man say maybe ten words.

"War is good for business," Davies said tartly.

"But bad for them that fights in it," Bill said. Through his binoculars, he saw one of the floating tanks flip and go under, sinking beneath the waves. "*Wellington* just went down to Davy Jones's locker!" he called.

Lieutenant Walter Lewis, Bill's tank commander, leaped up on top of *Achilles* and took Bill's binoculars.

Lewis was career army. He wore a thin black mustache on his upper lip and smelled of tobacco from the pipe he kept almost permanently lit. He clenched his pipe in his teeth now as he cursed. "And there go *Indefatigable* and *Mamma's Boy!*"

Even without the binoculars, Bill could see the tanks disappearing one by one beneath the waves. None of them made it to shore. Bill anxiously scanned the waves, worried the crews had drowned. He thought he saw the heads of surviving tank crewmen popping up in the water, but it was hard to be sure.

"Time to float the tanks!" one of the navy boys called down from the boat's tiny bridge.

"Oh no it isn't!" Lieutenant Lewis said. He thrust the binoculars back in Bill's hands and leaped from the top of the tank to the ladder up to the bridge. "Damn your eyes, man, can't you see what happened to the rest of the tanks? You've got to take us all the way!"

Bill couldn't hear the argument on the bridge, but he could tell the navy boys were scared. And well they should be. Bill could see the smoking remains of landing craft that had been hit by the German 88s and mortars. This boat's crew didn't want to get any closer than they had to. But Bill could also see the explosions on the beach, heard the drum of the machine-gun fire across the waves. There were hundreds of Allied soldiers on the beach—*thousands*—and they were dying left and right.

Bill thought of William the Conqueror and the invasion of England from France in 1066. *That* William had brought with him something like ten thousand men, three thousand of them on horses. Bill figured that he and his tank crew were like the British Army's cavalry. Bill's regiment—the Royal Dragoons—had even started as a mounted infantry unit in the 1920s before switching from horses to tanks for the Second World War. William the Conqueror couldn't have won the Battle of Hastings without his cavalry, and the Allies weren't going to win D-Day without their tanks. They needed the Royal Dragoons, but all the rest of them had sunk. The three tanks on this boat—his tank, *Achilles*, and the other two, *Valiant* and *Coventry's Revenge*—were the only ones left in the whole sector.

Lieutenant Lewis came back, packing tobacco into his pipe, and Bill knew that meant business.

"First the damn fool wanted to let us off here to drown. Then he threatened to turn around and go back out to sea!" Lieutenant Lewis said. "Said we've drifted too far west. Might end up on the British beach at Gold, where we belong, or on the Yankee beach at Omaha, or somewhere in between. I told him we were going to land on *some* beach, by God, and that he was going to take us all the way in! Get *Achilles* fired up. We're going in!"

ACHILLES

Bill climbed down into the American-made Sherman tank with the others. The space inside was tight for five people, but they each had room to do their jobs.

Bill was the driver, with a seat right up front and a tiny periscope to see through. Beside Bill, Thomas worked the .30-caliber front machine gun. Lieutenant Lewis sat with his head out a hatch at the top, the tank's real eyes and ears. Davies sat in the gunner's seat in the turret, and Murphy, his loader, sat right behind him with a hundred tank rounds under his feet.

They called their tank *Achilles*, after the Greek hero who'd been made invulnerable when his mother dipped him in the river Styx. They were hoping that invulnerability carried over to them too.

Bill turned the ignition. *Achilles* belched exhaust and roared to life, and he felt that good deep-down rumble in his stomach that told him the tank was alive. In front of them and behind them, *Coventry's Revenge* and *Valiant* revved their engines too.

"Think we'll make it to Bayeux?" Thomas asked Bill over the growl of the engine. "Get a look at the Bayeux Tapestry?"

Just the thought of it made Bill's skin prickle. The Bayeux Tapestry was a long, embroidered cloth sewn almost nine hundred years ago that told the whole story of William the Conqueror's Norman invasion of England. Bill had a shelf full of books about it at home, complete with color pictures. Knowing how much he loved to pore over them, Bill's wife, Maggie, had hand-embroidered his favorite scene—the part where William's horse falls but William lifts his helmet to signal to his troops that he is still alive, a perfect reproduction down to the last stitch!—and presented it to him just before he left for the war. With luck, Bill's path up and off the beach and into France would take him right through the city where the real tapestry was kept, and he would see the thing live and in person himself.

"I'd dearly love to see it, I would," said Bill. "So long as those lousy Krauts haven't nicked it and scarpered off to Berlin with it. But the French town I'd really like to get to is Amiens."

"What does Amiens have to do with William the Conqueror?" Thomas asked.

"Not a thing that I know of," said Bill. "But it has everything to do with me dad, Jack the Conqueror." Bill smiled, remembering. "He was a tank driver just like me, in the First World War. Fought in the Hundred Days Offensive, he did. And one day while they stopped for an oil change he carved 'Jack Richards was here 1918' on a stone. I'd surely like to find that stone and carve 'Bill Richards was here 1944' on it, just below me dad's name."

Bill nodded to himself. For the rest of his crewmates, today was Operation Neptune—the Allied invasion of Normandy. But for Bill, today was the start of what he'd come to think of as "Operation Amiens"—his mission to survive until he could find the very stone his father carved his name into.

"How touching," Davies said from above. "And I suppose twenty-five years from now, *your* son will come back during the *Third* World War and add his name too."

"Haven't got a son yet," Bill said, "though me dear wife, Maggie, was expecting our first when I shipped out. Won't know if it's a boy or a girl for another three months. If it *is* a son, I expect he'll follow in me footsteps, the way I've followed in me dad's."

"If there's another war," Thomas said.

"There's always another war," said Davies.

"Look alive down there!" Lieutenant Lewis called down to them. "We're almost onshore."

Bill rocked with *Achilles* as the boat hit the sand. Through his periscope, he could just see the coxswain, the navy boy whose job it was to drop the ramp in front. The coxswain yanked on the door release, and the ramp fell down. Almost immediately, the inside of the transport boat was riddled with bullets. The coxswain was hit and went down, and bullets pinged off *Coventry's Revenge*.

Bill cringed. *We're in the soup now for sure, all right*, he thought.

Coventry's Revenge charged down the ramp, hitting the waves with a splash and storming up and to the right.

"Full ahead!" Lewis yelled.

Bill heaved both levers forward, and *Achilles* roared out into the battle.

THE WRONG BEACH

The boat deck shifted uneasily beneath them, and Bill fought to keep *Achilles* on target. He was watching the tank ahead of them storm its way up the beach when—*shiiiii-BOOM!*—a shell from a German 88-mm gun slammed into *Coventry's Revenge*, and the tank exploded from the inside out.

Bill jumped out of his seat, clanging his head against his hatch. Beside him, Thomas yelled out an obscenity.

"Hard left! Hard left!" Lieutenant Lewis cried.

That was the direction Bill had been headed. *Coventry's Revenge* to the right, *Achilles* to the left, *Valiant* up the middle. That was the plan. But now the burning remains of *Coventry's Revenge* were half in Bill's way.

Each stick controlled the direction of the tank treads on that side, and Bill turned by pushing one stick forward and pulling the other backward in reverse. He could turn *Achilles* on a shilling if he needed to. Bill yanked back on his left stick and pushed forward with his right and heard the metallic groan as *Achilles* sheared along the side of what was left of *Coventry's Revenge*.

"Full ahead now!" Lewis cried. "Turret a quarter right!"

Bill drove *Achilles* up the beach. Thomas was awfully quiet and still beside him, and Bill saw with a quick glance that the color had drained from his friend's face. Thomas hadn't ever been in a real battle before, and what he was seeing and hearing clearly had him spooked.

"It was me dad who got me interested in the Bayeux Tapestry in the first place," Bill said.

"Hunh?" Thomas said.

"Me dad," Bill said, trying to distract his co-driver from the horror going on outside the tank. "I never did take to me studies in school, but I loved them books me dad had about the invasion and the tapestry."

"It's—it's not really a tapestry, you know," Thomas said. Some of the color had come back into his face, and he seemed to return to his senses. He put his eye to his gun sight and fired at a German emplacement on the cliffs. "Even though it's called a tapestry, it's more like embroidery. Ladies' needlework."

Bill knew that, but it was good to get Thomas talking again, thinking about something else besides *this* battle.

"Hell's bells, it's a slaughterhouse out there," Davies said, ignoring the both of them as he swiveled the big gun. "And I think we *are* on the wrong beach, sir. Those look like Yank uniforms."

"Then we'll help our American cousins get up and off the beach," Lewis said.

A mortar explosion struck right in front of the tank. It didn't rattle Bill—he felt insulated inside the four armored walls of the tank, like he was untouchable. Invulnerable. But seeing *Coventry's Revenge* go up like that right out of the gate had clearly fazed his co-driver. Poor Thomas jumped and ducked at every *ping* and *boom*.

"What I like about the Bayeux Tapestry," Bill said, hoping to calm his friend—and himself—"is that it's got everything. Generals and knights. Horses and boats. Cities and castles. Priests and doctors."

Someone screamed outside, the unmistakable cry of someone dying in pain.

"And—and things you wouldn't expect in a war story too," Thomas added, playing along with Bill. "Like ladies and dogs and cows. Halley's Comet even shows up in it, though they call it a star."

"Will you two clodpoles shut up about the bloody Bayeux Tapestry already?" Davies demanded.

"*Valiant*'s stuck!" Lieutenant Lewis reported. "She's having to back into the water and come ashore again."

Two tanks down, one left. So it's Achilles *versus the world now*, Bill thought.

Bullets pinged off the tank, and mortars exploded nearby, but none of that fazed Bill. He knew they wouldn't even ding *Achilles*'s armor. It was the big gun on the cliff they had to worry about.

"I see it! The German 88!" Lewis yelled down. "It's pointed at the beach and encased in a concrete bunker!"

The long stretch of beach they were attacking ran east to west, with tall cliffs at each end hiding German gun emplacements. Most of the emplacements pointed toward the sea, to repel ships, but at least one—the one that had taken out *Coventry's Revenge*—was aimed at the beach.

"Range: seven hundred yards!" Lewis called.

"Seventy-five millimeter!" Davies yelled to his loader.

"Up!" Murphy yelled.

"I've got it!" Davies said, sighting the German gun emplacement through his view scope.

"Fire when ready, Davies!" Lewis yelled.

Bill braced for the kick and crash of *Achilles*

launching a 75-mm shell a quarter of mile away, but—
THOOM!—something hit his tank first, lifting the
Sherman off the ground and tossing everyone around
inside like bowling pins.

BURSTING BOWELS

Thomas slammed into the wall and dropped to the floor. Davies fell out of his seat, and Murphy grunted as tank shells fell over and rattled around. Bill just managed to hang on to the control rods in front of him.

"What the devil hit us?" Davies asked.

"I don't know," Bill said, wrenching at the controls. "But I've lost steering on the left side!"

The others collected themselves, and Lieutenant Lewis picked up his pipe and climbed back up through his hatch on top for a look. "There aren't any guns in range to the east!" he yelled, as confused as the rest of them.

Throwing caution to the wind, Bill flung open the hatch above his head and peeked over the side. There was a huge crater in the sand, half underneath *Achilles*, and inside the crater lay the snarled remains of the tank's left tread.

Bill slithered back inside as bullets whizzed by. "A mine!" he told the crew. There was no way they could have seen it buried there, and the soldiers running around outside weren't heavy enough to set it off. Only a tank's weight could have activated it. "We've thrown a tread!"

Up top, Lewis cursed. "Did nobody remember Achilles was killed by an arrow in his heel?" he said bitterly.

"That's better than William the Conqueror," said Bill. "When he died, he was too fat for his coffin, you know, and when they tried to squeeze him into it, his bowels burst. The stench of it drove everybody from the room."

Murphy was helping Thomas bandage his head, but they both paused to stare at Bill.

"Turret still works, sir!" Davies said, readjusting his aim.

Bill looked up hopefully with the rest of them.

"Fire when you've got it!" Lieutenant Lewis yelled.

A moment's hesitation, and then: *P-TOM*. Bill felt the familiar kick as *Achilles* recoiled, rocking slightly over the hole under its left side. Bill was usually focused on driving, changing course after the shot had been fired, but now all he could do was sit and listen for the report.

There was a muffled *poom* in the distance, and Lieutenant Lewis swore again.

"Too low," he said.

"That's as high as she'll go," Davies said. "We need more elevation."

Shhhh-THOOM. Bill flinched as something big exploded a few dozen yards away, showering *Achilles* with sand and rock.

"The German 88. They're shooting back at us," Lieutenant Lewis said, cool as the River Mersey in February.

Bill shivered, truly afraid for his life for the first time that day. That German gun had taken out *Coventry's Revenge* in a single shot. As soon as it had *Achilles* in range, they were goners, and they all knew it. They were sitting ducks. But to abandon the tank with everything else going on outside was just as absurd. They had to take out that German 88 before it took *them* out.

Davies smacked his turret controls. "I just can't aim any higher! Not from here!"

No, Bill thought. *It can't end like this. Not before I get to Amiens!* There had to be a way to dig themselves out of this hole they'd gotten themselves in.

That was it!

"The sand—the crater!" Bill cried. "Sir! If we dig out from under the tank, the barrel will shift higher! Half the work's already done for us!"

"Richards, Owens-Cook, get out there and do it!" Lewis ordered.

"Me?" Bill said. He hadn't meant to volunteer.

"Us?" said Thomas.

"You're the drivers, and the one thing the tank *can't* do is drive anymore. That makes the both of you redundant," Lieutenant Lewis said. "Now hurry!"

DIGGING A HOLE

Bill muttered his first curse of the day and grabbed a shovel hanging on the wall of the tank. There was no way he and Thomas together could dig out enough sand to shift *Achilles* in time, even if they *weren't* shot. Not without the rest of the tank crew to help. But if everyone else came with them, there'd be no one to aim and fire the gun if they *did* manage to shift the tank.

We're completely and utterly jaspered, thought Bill.

Bullets pinged against the side of the tank as Bill crouched beneath the hatch, gathering his courage to go outside. Ever since he'd joined the army, he'd done what he could to follow in his father's footsteps. Become a tank driver. Get shipped off to France. Fight Germans. Getting to Amiens to see that stone his father had carved his name into had become an obsession. No—an *expectation*. Bill had known he was going to see that stone sure as eggs in April. But now that dream was crumbling faster than King Harold's defenses at the Battle of Hastings.

Another mortar exploded nearby, and Bill shook off his woolgathering. What he wanted and what he got were never the same thing, not since the day he was born. He was here, and he had a job to do. If he didn't get outside the tank this instant, he was going to die inside it the next.

Bill gave Thomas a nod, let out a quick jet of breath, and climbed out the hatch.

Outside, the world was bright and full of death. Bodies rolled in the surf. Men cried out for medics. Machine guns peppered the sand. Black smoke still poured from *Coventry's Revenge*, choking the air, and *Valiant* was still struggling to come ashore.

Bill slithered over the side of the tank as quick as he could and dove into the sand.

He landed on a soldier instead.

Two soldiers. Three. Hands grabbed him and helped right him, and Bill found himself staring at more than half a dozen American soldiers. They filled every inch of space behind the tank.

"Hey, I'm Dee," one of the Yanks said, holding out a hand to shake. "Welcome to the party."

Bill took the Yank's hand and shook it, still stunned. "Bill Richards. Liverpool, England."

Thomas slid over the edge of the tank into the crater, and this time the Yankee soldiers were ready for him.

"What the devil are you all doing here?" Thomas asked the Americans.

"You make a pretty great bunker against those German machine guns, bub," a soldier said.

"We were hoping to follow you all the way up the beach," said the soldier named Dee.

Bill frowned. He had to dig a hole and they were in his way! But then he realized how brilliant this was.

Every Yank had a shovel on his pack.

"We have to dig the sand out from under this side of the tank to give it enough elevation to hit that big German 88 on the ridge!" Bill told them.

That was all they needed to hear. Bill and Thomas started digging while the others pulled out their shovels, and soon they had *Achilles* shifting back, back, back in a flurry of sand.

"Good lord, Richards, how many of you are there down there?" Lewis called from the top.

"Just William the Conqueror and his army, boss!" Bill called back.

Thomas paused, wiping the sweat from his brow. "Bill, I know how much you love the Battle of Hastings and all that," he said. "But at the end of the Norman Invasion, it's the *English* who are defeated and flee the battlefield. Aren't you afraid history will repeat itself, and the Allies will lose?"

"No, but it's the other way round, see?" Bill said. He leaned on his shovel to catch his breath. "The English might have lost then, but it's the *invaders* who won. That's the important thing. And that's who the English are this time. We're the invaders!"

They both got back to digging. Bill caught the strange looks their conversation was getting from the Americans, and smiled.

Thomas laughed. "Between you and your father talking about the Norman Invasion all the time, it's a wonder your mother didn't come after you both with a rolling pin."

"Oh, I never met me dad," said Bill. "He died at Amiens."

Thomas froze. "What? But . . . the stone he wrote on, your fascination with the Battle of Hastings . . ."

Bill nodded, understanding Thomas's surprise. He hadn't explained before. "I inherited me love of the Norman Invasion from me dad—literally," Bill said. "He left me all his books. And me name, which he gave to me before he left. I was still in me mother's belly at the time. As to the stone with his name on it—well, he wrote to us about that in the last letter he sent before he died, didn't he?"

Thomas didn't ask any more questions.

"What about your old man?" Bill asked, still digging. He was wearing thin, but they were close. So close. "What'd he do in the last war?"

"He didn't fight," Thomas said quietly. He stopped shoveling for a moment. "He was a member of Parliament, so he didn't have to. But he was happy enough to send men like your father to their deaths. I'm sorry."

"Aw, not to worry. It's always us poor folks who does the dirty work. But you and Davies are top-drawer, and here you are up the creek just like the rest of us."

Shhhh-THOOM.

The beach on the other side of *Achilles* erupted in a geyser. Bill and the other diggers ducked as sand and rock showered them, and Bill caught his breath. The German 88 had fired again and just missed them. They had their range now though, Bill was sure. One more shot from the German gun, and they were all dead—everyone inside *and* outside the tank.

Bill and Thomas dug for all they were worth, and the American soldiers took up the cause with gusto.

"Just a little more—a little more—" Lieutenant Lewis coaxed them from the top of the tank. "There! Stop!"

"Get down!" Bill told the other diggers, and they flattened themselves in the crater and put their hands over their heads.

P-TOM. Achilles roared again, belching fifteen pounds of lead and TNT at two thousand feet per second toward its target. In a moment there was another *poom*, and this time Bill heard Lieutenant Lewis and the others inside the tank cheering.

"You did it, Richards! By God, you did it!" Lieutenant Lewis cried. "Hit it again, Davies! Hit it again!"

Bill heard clanking inside as Murphy reloaded. The sound was overridden by a louder clanking sound running up toward them, and Bill peeked over the top of *Achilles* to see *Valiant* running up from the water's edge, sand flying from the back of her treads. He felt a rush of relief, and he and Thomas exchanged a grin.

With a whoop, the American diggers tossed their shovels aside and ran for the moving shelter of *Valiant*, following it up and off the beach.

Bill stood, took off his beret, and waved at the Yanks.

"If you get to Bayeux before us, look out for the tapestry!" he called. "The one about the Norman Invasion!"

"Next stop, Bayeux," Thomas said, standing up and putting a hand on Bill's shoulder. "And then Amiens."

"Just like me dear old dad," said Bill.

OPERATION NEPTUNE

JUNE 6, 1944

MIDMORNING

OMAHA BEACH

VALIANT

Dee jogged along in a crouch with the other soldiers, staying in the protective lee of *Valiant*, the tank that had thankfully come up from the waterline to escort them higher up the beach. He turned to look at the two English soldiers who'd emerged from *Achilles* to dig the hole with them, and the one with the funny accent waved goodbye with his hat. What was his name again? Bill?

"If you get to Bayeux before us, look out for the tapestry!" Bill called. "The one about the Norman Invasion!"

Dee didn't have any idea what he was talking about, but he smiled and waved back anyway.

Dee saw the other English soldier say something and put a hand on Bill's shoulder, and then—

KRA-KOOM!

Achilles exploded in a towering ball of smoke and flame, throwing bits of metal shrapnel everywhere. The blast knocked Dee on his back, and he had to be helped up by another soldier.

"No!" Dee cried. *No—the tank crew!*

But how? They had taken out the big German gun! Then Dee saw it—*another* German gun, in a bunker up on the cliffs in the other direction. Just close enough to the other big gun to cover the entire beach between them. Dee's heart sank. *Achilles* had taken one of the guns out, but not both.

Dee scanned the raging bonfire that had been the *Achilles*, trying to find anyone who had survived. But there was nothing. Whoever had been inside the tank, and the two soldiers who had dug out the crater with him—they were all dead.

What were their names? Where were they from? Who had they left behind in England who would mourn them when they didn't come home?

Bill. The friendly one's name was Bill, and the tank was called *Achilles*. Dee knew that much. Bill and *Achilles*. Dee would remember them the rest of his days.

He just hoped "the rest of his days" wasn't *today*.

Valiant took Dee and the other soldiers as far as it could, but Dee still wasn't all the way up the beach. The German machine guns peppering the Sherman tank might as well have been on the moon for all that Dee could reach them yet. Between the high cliffs and the waterline, the Germans had built a concrete seawall. It was five feet tall and topped with concertina wire—coiled metal wire with razors along it every few inches.

The seawall was a deadly obstacle but a kind of shelter too. Dee saw that dozens of American soldiers had made it that far, and they now sat with their backs to it, protected from the German machine guns along the cliffs. To join them, Dee had to cross a distance of maybe ten yards—no more than a football first down. But that ten yards was littered with the bodies and equipment of all the American soldiers who *hadn't* made it. He caught quick flashes: Busted radios. Abandoned gas masks. Broken men crying out for their mothers. Rifles. Burning bodies, the smell so rancid Dee gagged.

Valiant started to back away.

Dee had to get to the seawall. Would he be hit with a hail of German bullets when he stepped out from behind the tank, or would their machine guns be trained somewhere else for the precious few seconds Dee needed to run ten yards? Who lived through this hell and who died, and why? Was it veteran experience? Divine providence? Dumb luck? Dee didn't know, and he didn't have time to figure it out. He took a deep breath, closed his eyes, and leaped out from behind the tank.

Bullets whizzed. Mortars exploded. Behind Dee, something big blew up near the water.

"Medic! Medic!" he heard a soldier scream.

Dee ignored them all and ran.

OPERATION INTEGRATION

JUNE 6, 1944

MIDMORNING

OMAHA BEACH

OPEN FOR BUSINESS

"Medic! Medic!" someone screamed, and Corporal Henry Allen looked up. While every other soldier on Omaha had been ordered to ignore the cries of the injured and wounded and get their butts up and off the beach as fast as they could, Henry's orders were the exact opposite. He *wasn't* allowed to leave the beach, not until the last of the fighting was over, and when somebody called out for help, it was his job to run through a hail of bullets to help them.

Corporal Henry Allen was a medic.

Mortars boomed as Henry stood and ran in the direction of the injured soldier.

Omaha Beach was covered with bodies. Most of them dead. Henry found the one among them who was still alive, the one who had called out for a medic, and dropped to a knee beside him.

The wounded soldier looked up at him through blurry eyes.

"Hey," the soldier said. "You're black."

Henry paused and pretended to examine his hands.

"My God," said Henry. "You're right. I hadn't noticed!"

Henry was twenty years old, with movie-star good looks. He had brown skin, big brown eyes, and short, dark brown hair. Above his lip he sported a pencil-thin mustache similar to the one Clark Gable wore in the film *It Happened One Night*.

As the soldier drifted into unconsciousness, Henry examined him, looking for injuries. Most of the soldiers on the beach, like Henry's patient, were white. All except the 320th Barrage Balloon Battalion, Henry's unit. The US Army was segregated. That meant that white soldiers and black soldiers didn't mix—except, of course, for the white officers *in charge* of the black battalions.

Henry had wanted to be an officer. He had been born and raised on the South Side of Chicago, Illinois, where his father was a postal carrier and his mother stayed home to take care of him and his sisters. He loved his family, but he had always wanted something more, and when he graduated from high school, he entered Lincoln University in Pennsylvania as a premed student. Then the war came, and he had applied for the army's

Officer Candidate School. He'd passed too. But the army told him they already had as many black officers as they needed. Which was hardly any. White soldiers didn't trust black soldiers to be officers, and didn't trust them to fight either.

So Henry decided to train as a medic instead.

Most black soldiers were support troops, driving trucks and bulldozers and loading equipment. Henry, a fully trained medic, was assigned to an all-black battalion, not a white one. He was there to take care of wounded black soldiers, but he sure as heck wasn't going to sit around when there were white soldiers to take care of too. He was a medic, and he was going to help anybody who needed fixing.

"So I guess we're integrated now," Henry said, more to himself than to his unconscious patient.

The soldier had a bullet wound to the shoulder, but he could be moved. Henry dragged him up toward the shell line at the crest of the beach. German bullets whizzed past Henry as he went, even though he was clearly wearing the white-and-red armband and the red cross on his helmet that marked him as a medic. The enemy wasn't supposed to do that. You weren't supposed to shoot at the other side's medics.

The Nazis aren't supposed to do a lot of things, thought Henry, *but they do them anyway.*

At the shell line, Henry found a small patch of sand

that had been dug out by a soldier and then abandoned, presumably when he charged farther up the beach. Henry unpacked a little lean-to tent with a red cross painted on it and set it up in the sand. Inside the tent, he laid out some of the equipment he'd brought with him in his two large medical bags: Disposable morphine syringes. Eye dressings. A field tourniquet. Gauze bandages and adhesive tape. Iodine. Plaster. Scissors. Thermometer. Pills to bring down fever. Sulfa powder to prevent infection. And paper tags for the wounded, to list what was wrong with them and what he'd done to help.

The first medical station on this patch of Omaha Beach was open for business.

BURST BALLOONS

Henry pulled his patient into his tent and examined him more closely.

Ordinarily, Henry's job as a battlefield medic in a combat situation like this would be to give a wounded soldier morphine to prevent shock, sprinkle sulfa powder on the wound to keep it from becoming infected, and bandage him up. The wounded man would then be loaded onto one of the empty landing crafts and taken back out to a medical ship at sea. But Omaha was a horror show. Everybody was too busy trying not to die to take the wounded away, and none of the landing crafts were hanging around long enough to load them up anyway. A bunch of the boats had hit mines and lay smoldering in the surf. Nobody was getting off this beach for a long, long time—not until they managed to get up and off it in the direction of Berlin. Which meant that Henry was going to have to do a little more than wrap people up in bandages.

Henry gave the soldier a shot of morphine and began to dig out the bullet in his shoulder with forceps.

Henry and the other men from the 320th Barrage Balloon Battalion were the first and only black combat unit in the whole Normandy beach invasion. Their mission had been to come ashore once the beach was mostly secure and install big gray blimp-shaped barrage balloons. Once up, the balloons were supposed to protect all the soldiers and support staff coming up off the beach into Normandy from enemy planes. The steel cables that held the balloons were hard for planes to see and even harder for them to dodge, and could rip off a wing or gum up a propeller.

It was unusual for the US Army to give such an important job to a black unit. The highly trained 320th Barrage Balloon Battalion was rare and exceptional, and Henry was proud to be a part of it.

Which would have been all well and good if the invasion had moved ahead like the generals planned. Omaha Beach was supposed to be in Allied control long before now, but it wasn't. Not by a long shot. As soon as the ramp went down on Henry's landing boat, he'd seen that for a lie. Hundreds of American soldiers still hid behind obstacles and lurked in the water. Men still ran for the shell line, the seawall, the protection of a burning tank, under withering machine-gun fire. Big German guns still destroyed landing boats, and mortars carved craters in the sand.

The whole Allied attack on Omaha was hopelessly stalled, but that hadn't stopped the United States Army from continuing to deliver new waves of soldiers like Henry and the 320th right on schedule. His unit's balloons had been shot by the Germans for target practice, and the soldiers of the 320th had scrambled to dig in and join the fight. Including Henry. Which was why he was here now.

A mortar shell hit close by, showering the top of Henry's tent with sand. He kept working, carefully extracting the bullet from the soldier's shattered shoulder. He almost tossed the slug away into the sand, then decided to slip it into the soldier's pocket instead. The wounded man might want it later for a souvenir.

Henry sprinkled sulfa over the wound and bandaged it up tight. The soldier was going to need a proper operation, and soon, but for now he was stable. Henry stuck the empty morphine syringe into a buttonhole on the man's tunic so the next medic would know how much painkiller he'd given him, and filled out a tag explaining the soldier's injury and what Henry had done about it.

Henry slid the soldier sideways out of the tent, laying his head just below the top of the shell line to keep him hidden from the German machine guns, and went off to find his next patient. Henry tried to ignore the fight raging all around him, hauling crying, moaning men back to his station again and again.

As a medic, Henry had been trained to keep his patients talking—in part to help them stay conscious, and in part to distract them from the sometimes-nauseating things he had to do to them. "Where ya from?" was the question all soldiers ended up asking each other when they first met, even if they were never going to see each other again. Henry, who loved movies, liked to ask everyone what their favorite film was instead. He got a lot of good ones that day—*King Kong*, *The Wizard of Oz*, *Frankenstein*, *The Thin Man*, *Robin Hood*, *Gunga Din*. All movies Henry had seen again and again in the theater. While he talked movies, Henry extracted bullets. Bandaged wounds. Sedated shock victims. There was more he wanted to do, more he *needed* to do for these men, but he only had a few basic, precious things in his medical bags and the worst possible conditions to use even those.

Henry was exhausted, but he kept working. What if he took a five-minute break—just five minutes—and in those five minutes a man died who Henry could have saved? How could he live with that on his conscience? No, he would keep working until he passed out or was shot dead.

Henry guessed it was close to noon by now, but he hadn't even taken a moment to look at his watch. Instead he dragged in another wounded soldier and sat heaving, trying to catch his breath, as he looked the man over for injuries.

"Well, I'll be a son of a gun," Henry said. He recognized this man.

"Of all the medical tents on all the beaches in all of France, he crawls into mine," Henry said, riffing off a line from one of his favorite movies, *Casablanca*.

The soldier's name was Lieutenant Richard Hoyte. He was a white soldier from Georgia. And he had made Henry's life in boot camp a living hell.

THE REAL WORLD

Henry's battalion had first been stationed at Fort Eustis, just outside Richmond, Virginia. Henry had been used to segregation in Chicago, but not the outright hatred he and the other black soldiers faced in the South. They got the worst barracks, the worst food, the worst equipment, and the worst assignments—all delivered with the vilest of racist slurs from the white southern officers put in charge of them.

Officers like Lieutenant Richard Hoyte, the man who now lay groaning on Henry's makeshift operating table on Omaha Beach.

Seeing Hoyte's face again made Henry remember that day one year ago when he and some of the other black soldiers had spent their day off from boot camp in downtown Richmond. It had been cold out—not Chicago cold, but there had been a bite in the air. The movie theater had been warm, at least, and there had been room in the colored section, which wasn't always the case. Most theaters reserved the balcony for black patrons, and once it was sold out, it was sold out, and black folks weren't allowed to sit downstairs with the white folks. The movie hadn't been all that bad either: a Hitchcock picture called *Saboteur*, with Robert Cummings and Priscilla Lane.

It was when Henry and the other black soldiers had tried to return to camp that things had gone wrong. Fort Eustis had buses that ran back and forth to town, and Henry and the others had arrived in plenty of time to catch the last bus back to base.

The bus was full, and they were sitting in the back waiting for it to leave when Lieutenant Hoyte led a team of military police on board and told Henry and his friends that they had to get off.

"Why?" Henry wanted to know.

"Because I said so, boy!" Hoyte spat.

Henry and the others hadn't thought that was a good enough reason, and had stayed put. This was the last bus back to camp that night. If they missed it, they'd technically be AWOL—"Absent Without Leave." Even if they caught the first bus back to camp the next morning, they would be in line for punishment for not returning to base on time.

Hoyte left the bus and came back with the local police, who threatened to throw them all in jail.

A jailhouse in Richmond, Virginia, was nowhere a black man wanted to be, even for one night, and Henry and the other black soldiers reluctantly got off the bus. They didn't know why they'd been kicked off in the first place until they got outside. Eight white soldiers had gotten there late and needed seats. They filed past Henry and the others and took the eight seats the black soldiers had just been forced to give up.

"That's not fair," Henry told Lieutenant Hoyte. "We were here first. Now we're going to get in trouble."

"Welcome to the real world," Hoyte had said with a grin.

So Henry and the other black soldiers had to spend the night on benches at the Richmond bus station. When they were finally able to catch a bus back to base the next morning, Lieutenant Hoyte had docked them a day's pay for being late.

Hoyte didn't seem to care what color Henry's skin was now though. He clutched desperately at Henry's arm.

"Doc," he rasped. "Doc, you gotta help me. My foot—"

Henry thought about all the ways he could get back at Richard Hoyte now. Tell him he didn't have any morphine left, and that the lieutenant was just going to have to tough it out. Tell him, "Sorry, eight other wounded soldiers are more important than you are, and I have to take care of them first," or "Sorry, Lieutenant, we're gonna have to wait for a white medic to take care of you."

But Henry knew he wasn't going to do any of those things. He was a medic, and he hoped to be a proper doctor one day. And doctors didn't let other people suffer, no matter how much they didn't like them.

Henry cut away what was left of Hoyte's right boot. Hoyte had stepped on a mine, and his foot was shredded. There was no way it could be saved.

"I can save your life but not your foot," Henry told him. "It's got to come off." It was the truth, and Henry took no pleasure in the telling.

Hoyte sobbed but nodded his understanding.

"I can't do it here," Henry explained. "I don't have a saw. But I'll give you something for the pain, and a tourniquet so you won't bleed to death first."

Henry dug out a morphine syringe, and Hoyte grabbed his arm again.

"Thank you, Corporal," Hoyte said, tears streaming down his face. "Thank you for coming to get me. I was sure I was going to die out there. You saved my life."

"Corporal," Hoyte had called him. Not "boy," not "spade," not "coon," nor any of the other horrible racist slurs Henry had heard from Hoyte and dozens of other white soldiers since he'd joined the army. When he'd needed to, Hoyte had seen Henry as a soldier, as a medic, as a *human being*.

Maybe, just maybe, Henry thought, this was a beginning. Maybe serving together, fighting together, living and suffering together, would make white people see black people as equals. Maybe, one day, white Americans and black Americans would eat together in the same restaurants. Maybe one day Henry would sit anywhere he wanted to sit in a movie theater, next to a white person, maybe, on the first floor. And maybe someday, the film they watched together would be a screwball comedy or an action adventure or a creepy monster movie with a black man as the main character, not the main character's servant or piano player.

Maybe one day, the white people of America would judge Henry by something other than the color of his skin.

A mortar exploded outside the tent, and Henry heard someone call for a medic.

Henry sighed. First they fixed Nazi Germany, then they fixed the United States.

No, Henry thought. *First I fix this foot.*

SUCKING CHEST WOUND

Henry left Hoyte in better shape than he'd found him: leg tied up to stop the blood loss, morphine injected for the pain, and lying comfortably beside Henry's other patients in the makeshift recovery ward along the shell line. Unless a mortar landed on top of Henry's Omaha General Hospital, Lieutenant Hoyte would live to tell the tale of the black medic who saved his life.

BOOM. Another mortar exploded nearby, and Henry closed his eyes and shook his head. He'd come to dread the sound of mortars. Not so much because he was afraid one would hit him, but because they were almost always followed by the inevitable cry of "Medic! Medic!"

Out Henry went again, into the bullets and explosions, picking his way through the dead in search of that one man who was wounded but still alive. Henry's training taught him that even a man who didn't call out for him might still be alive, might need his help to survive. But there were enough men yelling "Medic! Medic!" that he didn't have time to check on the ones who were silent. Not yet.

Henry shook his head and sighed. He didn't detest his job—he was glad to bring comfort when and where he could. He just hated what he saw when he got there.

The worst was when he found men who were still alive but wouldn't be for long. The ones he knew he could do nothing for. The ones who wouldn't even have stood much of a chance in a fully stocked emergency room at a hospital back in the States. As much as Henry wanted to, he couldn't give them morphine to make their last moments painless; he had to keep what painkillers he had on hand for the men he *could* save. All he could do for a mortally wounded man was put a hand to his chest, whisper "I'm sorry, pal," and move on.

"Medic! Medic!"

Henry stayed low, making sure his red cross armband and helmet were still visible. The call this time came from two white soldiers huddled behind one of the big X-shaped Czech hedgehogs that still dotted the beach. Henry went to his knees in front of them and diagnosed them visually. One of the two soldiers had burns on his right arm and the right side of his face.

The other one had no obvious injuries. The burn victim Henry could treat here on the spot without getting him back to his tent.

"You're a medic?" the one with the burns asked.

"I'm not running around on Omaha without a weapon for fun," Henry told him. "What's your name, soldier?"

"Bourke."

"All right, Private Bourke. I'm going to treat your burns with boric acid and wrap you up, and you should be good to go. What's your favorite movie?" Henry asked as he started to work.

"My favorite movie?" Bourke said. "I don't know. *Buck Privates*?"

Abbott and Costello join the army. "That's a good one," Henry said. "How about you?" he asked the other soldier.

"Any Western with—with John Wayne in it," he rasped.

Henry instantly looked up from what he was doing. There was something awfully wrong with the other man's breathing, but he didn't have any visible wounds.

"What's wrong with you, friend?" Henry asked.

"Nothing," the other soldier wheezed. "I'm just—worn out from running up through the surf."

That was entirely possible, Henry thought, but the way the man's fingers were turning blue said otherwise.

"Our Higgins boat got hit by a mortar," Bourke said. "Blew the whole thing apart. Robbins here was the lucky one. He got plastered right in the chest with a big piece of boat, but it didn't do nothing to him but knock him into the water. I got torched when the gasoline tank exploded."

"I don't think he was so lucky," Henry said. He finished putting the boric acid on Bourke's burns but didn't wrap them up yet. He turned to Robbins instead, running his hands along the man's tunic and underneath the webbing pouches on his chest to see if he could find any open wounds.

"I told you, Robbins wasn't hurt," Bourke said.

Robbins's fingers were still blue, and his breath still came short. Henry frowned. Private Robbins was showing all the symptoms of a sucking chest wound, but Henry couldn't find a chest wound.

Sucking chest wounds on the battlefield were common enough. You got one when something punched a hole in your chest—something like, say, a bullet—making a new pathway for air to get into your chest cavity. It was your chest cavity that was supposed to expand, not your lungs. The chest cavity pulled the outside of your lungs with it, filling your lungs with air pulled down your throat. But if something punctured your chest cavity, it could break that vacuum seal between your chest cavity and your lungs. Your chest would still move up and down like you were breathing, but your lungs would stay put and you'd suffocate. Worse, that space could fill up with air and actually *compress* your lungs, like exhaling underwater.

To fix a sucking chest wound, you slapped something airtight over the hole to plug it, like patching a tire. A piece of nylon cut from a GI's standard-issue rain poncho would do in a pinch. Henry had that.

What he didn't have was a hole.

"Hey," Bourke said. "Are you gonna wrap me up here, or what?"

Henry's hands went to the sides of Robbins's chest, and Robbins yelped.

There it is, Henry thought. Not a hole in his chest— there was still no external wound. But what about *internal*? What was it Bourke had said? Robbins was hit by shrapnel in the explosion. Robbins's pain was right where a rib might have broken, which could easily have punctured his chest cavity. Then the air from his lung would have filled his chest cavity instead.

Robbins didn't have a sucking chest wound—he had a collapsed lung.

"You're gonna have to wait," Henry told Bourke. "I need to operate on your friend *right now*."

A SECOND OPINION

Henry took a green canvas kit from his web belt and unrolled it on the sand. Tucked into the kit were scissors and a scalpel.

"Whoa whoa whoa!" Robbins wheezed, scooting back from the knives.

"Hey! What the hell are you doing?" said Bourke, moving next to his friend.

"You have a collapsed lung," Henry told Robbins. "I need to cut a hole in your side to release the air that's built up inside your chest cavity."

"*Cut a hole in my side?*" Robbins cried, then coughed.

The hole will close on itself, Henry thought. *What have I got that can keep it open and still let air out?*

Did he still have a glass syringe? The army had been taking them out of their medical kits in favor of much smaller, disposable plastic morphine syringes.

Bourke shoved Henry's shoulder, snapping him out of his reverie.

"Hey," said Bourke. "You ain't sticking no knife in Robbins. He's just exhausted. We all are! You don't know what you're talking about."

"And you do?" Henry said. "Where'd you go to medical school?"

Henry would never have said that to a white man back home, but he didn't have time to mess around. Robbins could barely draw a breath. Why wouldn't they just let him do his damn job?

"I'll give you morphine," Henry told Robbins. "You won't feel a thing."

Robbins still shook his head.

"Medic! Medic!" Bourke called.

Henry turned and saw who Bourke was calling to. Another medic was working his way from body to body in the surf, checking to see who was alive and who was dead.

A white medic.

The man hurried over and dropped to his knees behind the hedgehog.

"What's wrong?" he asked Henry. "Need an assist?"

"This fool wants to stick a knife in my buddy!" Bourke told the white medic.

The white medic did a quick appraisal of Robbins. He apparently came to the same conclusion that Henry first had—sucking chest wound—and immediately began feeling Robbins's chest for a wound.

The white medic frowned. "There's no wound."

"See?" said Bourke. "Tell him he's crazy."

"*In*ternal," Henry said.

The white medic's eyes went wide. "Broken rib?"

"I think so," said Henry.

"You'll definitely have to make an incision," the other medic said. "What are you going to use to keep the hole open?"

Henry held up an empty syringe he'd found in his kit. He'd pulled out the plunger and removed the needle, leaving a four-inch glass tube with a small hole on one side and a larger hole on the other.

"Smart," the white medic said.

"Wait, I didn't call you over to *agree* with him," Bourke said.

Storm clouds gathered on the white medic's face. "*You* called me over here?" he said to Bourke. His voice took on a hard edge. "Private, I want you to take a good look around this beach. Do you see the explosions? The bullets? *The bodies*? Do you see the boats that are dumping hundreds more soldiers into this meat grinder every minute? There's maybe one medic for every fifty wounded soldiers on this beach, one for every *hundred*, and you call me over *to get a second opinion*? What makes you think this man knows anything more or less about what he's talking about than I do?"

Bourke didn't answer. He didn't have to. They all knew why.

Because Henry was black.

"Now let me get back to my job, and let this man do his and save your buddy's life," the white medic said. "You're lucky he caught it. I don't think I would have." He turned to Henry. "You need any help?"

Henry shook his head. "Private Bourke's gonna help me. Right?"

Bourke nodded sheepishly and looked away.

"Good luck out here," the white medic told Henry.

"You too," Henry said. "And thanks."

It was a tricky procedure in the best of conditions, let alone with bullets and mortars and explosions all around them, but Henry made his incision and inserted the modified syringe tube while Bourke held Robbins in place. As soon as the syringe tube was all the way in, there was an audible hiss of air escaping, and Robbins took his first full deep breath in fifteen minutes. There was still a pretty good risk of infection, but the private wouldn't have lived long enough to get an infection if Henry hadn't done what he did.

"All right, Robbins," Henry said. "Your D-Day is over. When those boats start taking people back out and aren't just dumping new soldiers on shore, you call a medic over and get yourself back to a hospital ship. They'll clean you up and send you back to England, where you'll get some R & R and a pretty Purple Heart for your troubles."

Henry finally put the bandages over Bourke's burns. "You," Henry said to Bourke, "you're not done yet. But you've got to leave your buddy behind. He's gonna be okay."

"I hear ya," Bourke said. "Thanks, Doc. I'm sorry."

Henry rolled up his instrument kit. "Just go take out one of those German bunkers up there on the cliffs so they stop shooting at me, and we'll be even."

"Medic! Medic!" someone cried.

Bourke nodded, and Henry stood to run back out into the fray.

The man calling for help lay in the stretch of sand between the shell line where Henry had set up his station and the seawall farther up the beach. That patch was miles wide, but only about ten yards deep, and it was murder from the German machine guns.

Bullets sank into the sand all around Henry as he charged into the deadly no-man's-land. He dropped to his knees beside the white soldier.

"Medic," the boy mumbled. "Medic."

"Yeah, yeah, that's me," Henry said.

This patient was a big guy—well over six feet tall

and a couple hundred pounds. Long stubbly face, dark, curly hair, and shrapnel in his leg.

"What's your name, kid?" Henry asked.

"*Medic,*" the soldier moaned.

"No, *I'm* the medic," Henry said. "I'm going to patch you up and get you back in the fight. And yes, I already noticed I'm black."

OPERATION NEPTUNE

JUNE 6, 1944

AFTERNOON

OMAHA BEACH

PINNED DOWN

Dee watched as a bullet hit an American soldier not two yards away from him. The soldier twisted in the sand, still mid-run, and collapsed like a marionette. He wasn't alive long enough to call for a medic.

Dee didn't even flinch. He didn't cry. He didn't yell. He had seen something very much like that over and over and over again for the past few . . . few what? Minutes? Hours? How long had he been sitting here with his back against the seawall, listlessly watching the living nightmare on Omaha Beach?

He tried to think. He had left the British transport ship during night and fog. Arrived on the beach at dawn. A lifetime ago. The sun was high in the cloudy sky now.

Hours, then. That meant Dee had been here,

hugging his arms to his chest, shivering even though he wasn't cold, for hours.

Stretching out to his left and his right were all the other soldiers who'd been lucky enough to make it this far up the beach, to the protection of the seawall. There were hundreds of fallen, lifeless American soldiers in the short distance between the wall and the water. There were only forty or so here with Dee.

BOOM. A mortar exploded a dozen yards down the line, just this side of the seawall, taking out four or five of the men who'd been hiding there. If the mortar had been aimed just an inch or so to the right, it would be bits of Dee that were scattered all over the sand.

Dee would have shrugged, but he was too tired. It might be him next time. It might not. Now or later didn't really matter.

Sid was already dead. Sid, his best friend in the army—maybe the best friend he'd ever had in his entire life. All Sid had ever wanted was to fight the Germans. Back when they met in boot camp, Sid had told Dee about the day his synagogue in New York City had hosted a Jewish woman who'd managed to escape from Nazi Germany. She'd horrified the congregation with stories of how the Nazis destroyed Jewish homes and burned down their places of worship. How the Nazis segregated the Jewish people, deprived them—had even begun to murder them. Sid had wanted to go to war with Nazi Germany right then, but the United States wasn't *in* the war yet. Sid had been just about to run away to Canada to join the Canadian army so he could do *something*, when the Japanese had attacked Pearl Harbor and America had at last gone to war. Sid had enlisted right away and gotten himself shipped to Europe. But now he had died before he'd ever gotten his revenge on a single Nazi soldier. How was that fair?

A mortar exploded nearby, and Dee saw again in his mind's eye the blast that had taken out Sid. One minute Sid had been there, and the next he was gone. *That's the fate of every last man on this beach*, Dee thought. *We're all going to die here, and there's nothing any of us can do about it. We're all going to die without getting our chance for revenge.*

No one had made it up and off the beach yet. They were supposed to have taken the German bunkers on the cliffs and been miles inland by now, but they were still pinned down. Still dying from German machine guns and rifles and mortars and grenades. Dee wondered if the soldiers on Utah—the other American beach—or the men on any of the three British beaches—Sword, Juno, and Gold—had fared any better. Distantly, Dee hoped so. For their sake. There was no use hoping for anything here.

So stupid, Dee thought. *I was so stupid to think I was going to come here and change anything.* The time for changing anything in Germany was long gone. His family should never have left. They should have spoken up before things got this bad, even if it had meant disappearing into the Night and Fog. If everyone had spoken up at once, they couldn't have made them all disappear, could they?

But his parents had been scared. Scared for him, and scared for themselves.

They don't know what it really means to be scared, Dee thought now. Nobody but the people sitting against this seawall, nobody but the soldiers lying wounded and dead in the surf of Omaha Beach, had ever known true fear.

Another Higgins boat pulled up to the shore with another forty soldiers inside.

"No. Go back," Dee said. "Don't lower the ramp. Stay on the boat."

They couldn't hear him, even if he yelled. Not this far away. Not over the constant *rat-tat-tat* of the German machine guns. But Dee said it out loud as if the universe might hear him. As if by just speaking the words he could will it to happen.

"Don't do it," Dee said. "Don't drop the ramp. Don't drop the ramp."

They dropped the ramp.

Dee looked away as bullets ripped into the boat and row after row of soldiers fell screaming into the water.

"Go! Go!" a soldier a few paces off to Dee's left shouted, and Dee looked back up.

One of the soldiers from the boat, unbelievably, had run right down the ramp and into the knee-high surf without getting shot.

"The tank! Get to the tank, bud!" cried another soldier along the seawall.

Valiant, the tank that had given Dee the cover he needed to get this far, had long since become mired in the wet sand, its turret and machine guns aimed too low to do any good. But while it could no longer shuttle soldiers up and down the beach in its shadow, *Valiant* was now at least a valuable way station on the path to the seawall.

"The tank! Get to the tank!" Dee called.

There was still no way for the soldier down there on the beach to hear any of them, but somehow the solider spotted *Valiant* and ran for its shelter.

He made it! Dee sat up higher.

"The hedgehog," one of the other soldiers at the seawall said, willing the soldier to see the big steel obstacle a few yards away.

"No, the shell line—straight for the shell line!" said another soldier.

"He's moving!" Dee cried.

The soldier burst out from behind the tank, head down. He'd made his decision. He was running for the hedgehog.

"Go! Go! Run!" the soldiers at the seawall cried.

Dee ducked and cringed along with the running soldier, feeling his adrenaline, his fear. He was almost there—almost there! Then suddenly—*POOM!*—a mortar landed right on top of the hedgehog, blasting sand and shells and shrapnel all over the beach.

THE LUCKIEST SOLDIER ON OMAHA BEACH

The soldier just missed getting hit by the exploding hedgehog. He stumbled and fell, and Dee held his breath. Laden with gear, the soldier struggled to his feet. His hedgehog hiding place destroyed, he staggered off toward the shell line instead. *Go, go, go,* Dee prayed silently. Bullets kicked up sand beside the soldier, behind him, but still nothing hit him.

"This guy's the luckiest soldier on Omaha Beach," Dee whispered.

The soldier dove for the protection of the shell line, and he fell so fast, flopped so clumsily, that Dee thought he might have been shot after all. There were gasps up and down the line of soldiers at the seawall. Calls for the soldier to be okay. To not be dead.

The soldier peeked up over the shell line, and the line of soldiers at the seawall cheered. Dee let out the breath he'd been holding and smiled for the first time since hitting the beach.

The soldier put his head back down and waited. Dee knew what he must be feeling. They all did. The soldier had found a place of safety in the middle of the storm, no matter how slight it was, no matter how tenuous. Dee didn't yell for the soldier to get up, to leave the protection of the shell line. No one did. No one who had been through that hell—who had had to summon the courage to stand up again when he could just lie there forever and be safe, his face buried in the sand—could ask him to do that, because none of them had wanted to do it either. But they knew he would, in his own time. Because he had to.

Dee could feel the anticipation up and down the line as they waited for him to make his move. The suspense was electric. Other soldiers had crawled out of the surf, and some had even made it up to the shell line in other places, but it was this soldier—the Lucky Soldier—who had their attention. There was something special about him. Something untouchable.

Dee's breath came hard and fast. Did a German sniper have his rifle trained on the Lucky Soldier right now, waiting for him to do something? Was a mortar going to find him before he worked up his courage? Would a machine gun tear him apart the moment he stood?

They waited long, anxious minutes, none of them

calling out. None of them wanted to be the person who lured the Lucky Soldier to his death. But then, finally, the Lucky Soldier did what they all had done: He climbed to his feet and started his run across the ten yards that separated him from the seawall.

Dee and the others immediately roared their encouragement.

"Come on!"

"You can make it!"

"Just a few more steps now!"

"You're almost here!"

"You've got it! You've got it! You've got it!"

Dee stood, waving his arms, ready to pull the man in.

And then a bullet struck the Lucky Soldier, right down through his shoulder, straight down to his heart, and he tripped and fell face-first into the sand.

One of the other soldiers cursed. Another sobbed. Dee could only stare forlornly at the dead soldier a few feet away. He didn't think he could feel any lower, didn't think the black hole in his stomach could grow any larger, any deeper, but it did. It opened up and swallowed Dee whole, and he felt himself fading out of existence.

He had to *do* something. Do something right now or he would disappear forever.

What he did was run for the body of the Lucky Soldier.

SAY HELLO

The wet sand twisted under Dee's boots as he ran. Bullets still flew, and mortars still exploded, but no German up on the cliffs had seen him yet, or else he'd be dead.

In two steps, Dee reached the Lucky Soldier. He snatched up the man's hand—it was still warm—and pulled him hard. The wet clothes, the heavy gear, the man's limp, lifeless body: It was like running against the tide. Dee screamed, a primal howl of anger and frustration and strength, and before his cry even ended, he had dragged the body of the Lucky Soldier up to the protection of the seawall. Bullets *fwipped* into the sand where he and the Lucky Soldier had been, but he was safe again now.

Dee squatted next to the body like a catcher, breathing hard.

"What the hell did you do that for?" one of the other soldiers asked. "He's dead."

"I—I don't know," Dee said. How could he explain that if he hadn't done it, he'd be dead too? "It just felt like a shame for him to make it all this way and not get here in the end."

The other soldiers nodded. It had been a dumb thing to do, to run out there and get shot at again, but they all understood.

Down the line, a medic had been treating a fallen soldier in the no-man's-land between the shell line and the seawall. Now he was trying to stand with his shoulder under the arm of the injured man to help walk him to safety.

"Come on," Dee told the others. He ran crouching along the protection of the seawall, past soldier after soldier, each with the same thousand-yard stare he'd just had, until he came perpendicular to the place where the medic struggled just a few feet away. Heedless again of the German guns up on the cliffs, Dee ran straight out and put his shoulder under the wounded man's other arm. More soldiers ran to join him, and together they had the wounded man and the medic under the lee of the seawall before any of them had taken a bullet.

"Thanks, pal," the medic said. He was black, Dee suddenly realized.

"Name's Henry," the medic said, and Dee introduced

himself. "D?" Henry asked. "Just like the letter *D*? Hang on—you got some scrapes here I can wrap up for you."

Dee sucked in a breath as Henry dabbed iodine on a cut on his arm.

"There's a German film called *M*, just the letter *M*," said Henry. "Came out in the States a few years back with English voices dubbed over the German. But the main character in that's a bad dude. You don't want to be anything like him."

With a start, Dee realized he knew the film. He'd never seen it, but he'd seen the creepy movie posters when he was a boy.

In Berlin.

Dee tried to look away, irrationally worried that someone might somehow see the look of recognition in his face, but Henry held his chin and dabbed at it with a cotton swab.

"What are you doing?" Dee asked.

"You took a bullet to the left arm and had one graze your face too. Didn't kill you, but it's going to leave a scar."

Dee frowned. When had he been shot? He tried to put a hand to his face, to feel the wound, but the medic slapped his hand away.

"Don't touch it," Henry told him.

"I can't—I can't feel them," Dee said. "The places I got shot. Did you give me morphine?"

"No. That's the adrenaline," the medic said. "When it wears off, you'll feel them. I'm not going to give you morphine because that would dull you and you're not so badly injured you can't fight."

Fight? Dee thought. *Fight what?* There was nothing to fight. Just invisible bullets and mortars that dropped out of the sky. All the hopelessness that had held him rooted to the seawall just a few minutes ago came washing back over him now, and he sagged. What was even the point of Henry patching him up if he was just going to be killed a few minutes later?

"Hey, when you're done being pampered you could maybe say hello," said a familiar voice. Dee turned to see the soldier he'd helped Henry carry out of no-man's-land.

It was Sid!

THE DEAD
AND THE DYING

"Sid!" Dee cried.

Dee pulled Sid to his feet and wrapped him in a hug.

"Watch the leg! Watch the leg!" Sid said, laughing. "I missed you too, buddy. When that mortar went off, I thought I'd lost you for good."

"I thought I lost *you*!" Dee said. "I thought you were dead!" Dee couldn't believe it. He couldn't stop smiling. But Sid's leg— "Are you all right? Are you hurt bad?" he asked.

"Don't count me out yet. I told you, I'm not leaving till I kill a Kraut."

"Your buddy took some shrapnel from the blast," said Henry. "He'll be a little slower than everybody else. You might have to stay close, give him a hand every now and then."

Sid put his arm around Dee's shoulder and shook

him like a little brother. "You kidding? We're not getting separated again. Thirty years from now, me and Dee here are going to be taking the train back and forth from New York to Philly to watch the Dodgers and the Athletics in the World Series!"

"Medic! Medic!" another soldier cried out.

"Somebody's playing my song," said Henry, and with a tip of his helmet he ran back out onto the battlefield. Back out into the bullets and the mortars and the mines. Dee shook his head in wonder at the medic's courage and skill.

Before Dee could ask Sid anything else, a tall, thin lieutenant Dee had never seen before came down the line of men at the seawall. He was crouching low so the Germans couldn't see him. There was blood all over the breast of his uniform—his or somebody else's, Dee couldn't tell—and a white gauze bandage crossed his face diagonally, coming down out of his helmet to cover his left eye.

"We've got to get off this beach!" the lieutenant told them. "The only people here are the dead, and those who are going to die. If we're going to die here, we might as well take some Germans with us."

"I hear that," said Sid.

"A mortar blew a hole in the seawall a few yards down," the lieutenant said. "That's our way up and out. Now, let's get the hell off this beach!"

The lieutenant's name was Mendoza. He wasn't from Dee's unit, but that didn't matter anymore. There was no radio, no way of coming together but this, in small groups of survivors who had ended up hiding beside each other at the seawall. Dee was still scared, but he couldn't sit here and wait for death any longer. He had to *do* something. And now that Sid was back, he had someone to do it with.

"You ready to do this?" Dee asked Sid.

"Yeah," said Sid. "But I think you're forgetting something."

Dee didn't understand.

"A rifle? A weapon of some kind?" Sid said. "You might need something like that at some point soon."

Dee stared at his empty hands. Of course—what was he thinking? He'd dropped his rifle in the ocean right after he'd left the Higgins boat.

"Hang on," Dee said. He jogged back to where the Lucky Soldier lay, the man's rifle beside him on the sand. Dee took it for his own.

"Thanks, pal," Dee whispered. "And I'm sorry."

"Through the hole, everybody!" Mendoza cried. "Let's go!"

D. KAUFMANN

Dee ran with Sid through the hole in the seawall.
The air just beyond the wall was thick with smoke, and
Dee threw his arm up to cover his mouth and nose.

It was the dry seagrass on the dunes; the bombardment from the Allied battleships must have set it on
fire. It was a curse, and a blessing. Dee's eyes watered
so badly from the smoke that he could barely see, but
the German machine gunners apparently couldn't see
through the smoke either. They kept up a steady stream
of machine gun fire, but they missed more GIs than
they hit.

Dee reached the top of the bluff at last and crouched
in the seagrass until Sid caught up. Only about twenty
or thirty American soldiers had made it to the top of
the bluff, but it was a start.

"All right," said Lieutenant Mendoza. "Half of you go left, the other half of us will go right."

Dee and Sid joined the group led by Mendoza toward a concrete-reinforced bunker with big guns aimed at the beach.

Almost immediately they came upon a small trench with a tripod-mounted machine gun and soldiers with rifles. The Germans never heard the GIs coming, and the American soldiers blasted them with rifles and machine guns of their own and jumped into the trench. Dee took aim at one of the Nazi soldiers and shot him dead with his rifle. It was a slaughter, but nothing compared to what the Germans had been doing to them on the beach below for the last five hours.

The Germans. Dee paused for a second. He was German. His family were Germans. He had relatives who were German. He'd just killed one of his own countrymen. A boy his age.

The boy's helmet had fallen off as he died, and Dee could see the name written inside: *D. Kaufmann.*

D—was his name Dietrich too? Dee shivered. If Dee and his family hadn't left Germany, that boy could be him.

But they *had* left Germany. And even before that, his parents had been against Hitler. They hadn't joined the Nazi Party, even when their neighbors and coworkers and other family members pressured them to sign up. For whatever reason, this boy had taken a different path. He had agreed to serve in the Nazi army. He had accepted Adolf Hitler as his leader. D. Kaufmann *wasn't* Dee's countryman. Not then, when Dee himself had lived in Germany, and certainly not now that Dee lived in America. These were not his people. The American soldiers in the trench with Dee, *those* were his people. And when he got back home, he was going to make it official.

Dee was going to become a United States citizen.

Sid caught up, still slow on his injured leg. "Dang it!" he cried. "I didn't get to kill a single one of them!"

"You'll get your chance," Lieutenant Mendoza said. "We've still got that bunker to take. Go! Go! Go!"

THE WIDERSTANDSNEST

The bunker was made of gray reinforced concrete that reminded Dee of the concrete aqueducts in Philadelphia built to handle runoff rainwater. The bunker was flat on top, with rounded corners at the sides; Dee knew that it was what the Germans called a *Widerstandsnest*—a "resistance nest"—one of almost a hundred strongpoints built up and down the coast to repel an Allied invasion.

For the last five hours, this *Widerstandsnest* had done its deadly job without interruption, and Dee was ready to put a stop to it.

Dee and Sid came up behind the fortress with the other GIs. Two large black steel doors barred their entry into the bunker. The other side, facing the beach, was the business end of the resistance nest. Dee could hear the *chuk-chuk-chuk* of a big machine gun and the *poom* of its mortar from here.

Did the Nazi soldiers inside know Dee and the others were right outside? Were they waiting behind the door to mow them down?

The makeshift Allied platoon covered Dee as he pulled on the doors, but they were bolted closed.

"Anybody got any grenades?" Sid asked.

"Got something better," a soldier said. He ran up and fixed the door with the same kind of bomb Dee had seen engineers using to explode the mines on the hedgehogs at the beach. Everybody took cover. A few seconds later—*THOOM*—the big steel doors blew inward, crumpling like a chewing gum wrapper. There was a stunned silence from inside, and Dee and Sid didn't wait around for the Germans to figure out what had hit them. They charged inside, with the other soldiers hot on their heels.

The resistance nest was a series of low, small concrete rooms connected by tight, dark corridors. A German soldier emerged from one of the rooms, and Dee shot him. He rushed into the room where the soldier had come from and blinked in the bright light—he was suddenly standing outside. But not, because he was still inside the pillbox. A mortar cannon stood in the middle of the round room, and he understood. This room had no roof because the Germans used it to lob mortars at the beach.

A German soldier popped out from behind the cannon and raised a pistol.

Bang!

Dee flinched, but it was the German soldier who fell, dead from a rifle shot from one of the GIs standing behind Dee. Dee was surprised to see that it wasn't Sid. Where had his friend gotten to?

Gunshots echoed in the tiny corridors. Dee found Sid in the hallway, locked in hand-to-hand combat with a Nazi soldier. Dee raised his rifle, but—*BANG*—another GI shot the German dead.

"Agh! That one was mine!" Sid cried.

Dee pushed past his friend and burst into a big room at the front of the fortress, rifle blazing. There was a huge gun in the room—a 75-mm cannon trained on the beach below—and four Nazi soldiers on hand to load it and fire it.

The German soldiers fired back with pistols. Dee's stomach tightened in fear. One of the soldiers beside him was hit and went down. Was it Sid? No. Dee caught one of the Nazis with a bullet to the chest, and then there were more GIs in the doorway. They broke to either side and circled the big gun, pinning the Germans back in the far corner of the room. Rifles thundered in the concrete room, and the GIs finished off the Nazi gun crew without taking another hit.

Dee hurried back through the resistance nest, searching the rooms and corridors with the other soldiers. There was one more mortar, but it and its crew had already been taken care of. The Germans in this pillbox had been routed.

Dee found Sid back in the front room with the big gun, standing over the dead German soldiers in the corner.

"I didn't get a single one of them," Sid said. "Didn't kill *a single German soldier* in the whole damn place! Not one Kraut, all day long! What am I, cursed?"

Dee smiled at Sid and shook his head. He felt exultant. His heart was still thumping in his chest. *They had survived.* They had gotten up off the beach and attacked a German bunker, and they had won!

With a start, Dee realized this must have been the big gun that had taken out the tank he'd helped shovel out of the sand. Bill's tank—*Achilles*. Dee remembered Bill, sadly. But at least he'd gotten revenge for him. Helped take down the Nazis who had killed the brave tank crew.

Dee peered out the bunker's window on the beach. Through the thinning smoke, he could see the place they'd just come from, and his happiness wore off quick.

Tanks burned. Half-tracks and jeeps lay swamped in the surf. Landing craft were caught on obstacles and blew up as they hit mines. Mortars geysered sand and water. Dead bodies dotted the beach like stones.

But things were starting to look more organized too. A tank was rolling off a landing craft, right onto the sand. Troops were moving up through the seawall in at least three places Dee could see, and as he watched, a controlled explosion took out the barricades blocking one of the roads off the beach. The battle continued.

Dee saw another German bunker to the west, just across a narrow river that drained into the sea. The German resistance nest was still hammering the beach with a big gun like the one Dee and the others had captured. But the big gun they had taken wasn't set up to shoot at this other one. Theirs could only reach the beach and the sea.

Dee considered rallying some troops and heading for the other bunker, but that wasn't their mission. Their orders were to get up off the beach and push inland. It had taken them far longer to get off the beach than anyone had thought, and at a far greater cost. But they had done it. Now it was on to the villages between here and Bayeux. They would have to leave the cleanup of Omaha Beach to the people who followed them.

"Come on," Dee told Sid. "D-Day ain't over yet."

GHOST TOWN

Dee and Sid hid behind one of the tall hedgerows that lined the fields and roads of Normandy. The sun was setting, and the sky was orange like fire. All around them were more American soldiers—perhaps two dozen—from different divisions. Most of them had bandages on their heads or arms or legs, sometimes self-treated, sometimes fixed up by medics along the way. All of them were survivors of Omaha Beach. And their reward for living through that hell? Now they got to push on into Normandy, freeing French towns from Nazi control on their way to the city of Bayeux. At Bayeux they would finally rest and regroup.

But first they had to clear this town. On both sides of the road were little houses built in a French style Dee was starting to recognize: two-story, flat-faced rectangular buildings made of light gray stone, lined with windows and topped with a black roof. Each little house had at least one chimney, but none of them were smoking.

Beyond the houses was a row of cafés and restaurants, and at the heart of the village, looming over everything else, was a tall gray medieval stone church with buttresses on the outside and a clock tower sticking up out of the middle. On another summer evening, it might have been a sleepy little picture-postcard French town. Dee didn't know the town's name, and he didn't think any of the officers around him did either. It didn't matter. It was a French town in German-occupied territory, which made it dangerous.

"I don't see any Krauts," Sid whispered. He still hadn't killed any German soldiers, and he was noticeably anxious.

"I don't see *anybody*," Dee said. The town was silent as the grave.

"Come on," said Sid. "Let's go find us some Germans."

"No, Sid—wait!" Dee called, but Sid had already jogged off in a low crouch for the first house. Dee was scared, but he hurried after him. Lieutenant Mendoza signaled for other soldiers to do the same.

Sid ran around the back side of the house and leaned against the wall beside a door. Dee propped himself up on the other side. Sid held his rifle in one hand and his other grabbed the doorknob. Dee counted down soundlessly, using his fingers. *Three, two, one—*

Sid threw the door open and entered the house, rifle at the ready, and Dee followed him in. Dee expected shots, yelling, *something*—but the house was silent and still.

They were in a small, unadorned kitchen. Pots and pans hung on the wall over a white enamel oven that stood on ornate metal legs. A pot with some kind of broth in it sat on the stovetop, beside a tall teakettle. Against another wall stood a dark brown wooden cabinet that Dee guessed held more cooking utensils. A small door led to an empty pantry.

Dee opened the oven door and felt heat radiate from it.

"Still warm," he whispered.

Sid nodded and crept into the next room. It was a small dining room with white floral wallpaper. A shelf with a few old books hung above a side table with faded photographs in frames. Another cabinet held plates, glasses, and silverware, and in the center of the room was a table just big enough for four chairs. A white tablecloth with a flower print covered the table, where there were plates and utensils for three people. There were half-eaten pieces of bread on each plate, and some kind of thin vegetable broth sat untouched in a ceramic tureen. Two of the chairs were pulled out from the table, and one had fallen over backward and still lay on the floor.

Sid and Dee shared a look. Both of them understood what they were seeing. Someone had been in the middle of eating a meal here and then left in a hurry. But who? A French family, or German soldiers? And where were they?

Dee lifted the fallen chair back up and stood it on its legs. He didn't know why he did it, but it felt proper to put it back to rights.

Sid and Dee split up and searched the house. In one of the second-floor rooms, Dee found a small bed with a stuffed bear tucked under the covers. Had place number three at the table been set for a small child? If so, *where were they*? There was no one upstairs, or down in the basement.

Dee and Sid rejoined the other soldiers outside. More of them had been through the other houses and found much the same thing—signs of life followed by a hasty retreat.

"It's a ghost town, Lieutenant," one of the privates said.

"Let's keep moving," Mendoza said. "But be careful."

Dee and Sid inched down the street toward the church, staying close to the houses.

Pa-CHOOM!

A house exploded on the other side of the street from

where Dee and Sid stood, throwing shattered stone and wood and glass everywhere. Four soldiers were killed in an instant, including Lieutenant Mendoza, and three more were critically wounded. As the GIs tried to drag their injured comrades to shelter, German machine-gun fire opened up on everyone, on both sides of the street. Dee's heart stopped. It was an ambush!

An engine roared to life, drowning out the sound of the German snipers. An engine louder than any Dee had ever heard in his life. It snarled like a living thing. Like some monstrous lion.

Clank-clank-clank-clank-clank.

The thing crawled out of the shadow of the church at the end of the street, and Dee's eyes went wide.

"Panzer!" Sid cried.

The village was protected by a German tank.

PANZER

Dee and Sid dragged an injured soldier to cover in the alley between two houses, and Dee peeked around the corner. He'd seen Sherman tanks, of course—up close and personal—but he'd never seen the legendary German panzer before.

Panzer meant "armor" in German, and though there were different versions, most American GIs called anything that resembled a tank with a black German cross on it a panzer. This one was painted a light gray, had massive metal tracks that clanked and rattled as it ran, and featured a snub-nosed cannon sticking out of the turret on its top. That little cannon was a 75-mm gun that could do a lot of damage—like punch through the armor of an Allied tank. Or blow up a French house.

Pa-CHOOM!

The tank fired again, and another wall of a house

exploded. Dee felt helpless. His rifle wouldn't do anything against that panzer's armor. Neither would anyone else's.

"Bazooka! Anyone got a rocket launcher?" a sergeant yelled. But no one had made it off the beach with one.

"Satchel charge!" cried the sergeant.

A soldier slapped down an empty satchel, and another soldier threw a small block of C-2 explosive inside. Someone else contributed a grenade to act as the detonator. Now all they needed was someone to run out and toss the satchel onto the tank.

Time slowed for Dee. In his mind's eye he was suddenly a little boy again, holding his mother's hand as they boarded a boat in the middle of the night, frightened by his parents' fear but excited for the adventure as they snuck out of Germany. All to save him, they explained, from having to put on brown shorts and a brown shirt and a red-and-black armband and join the Hitler Youth, which had looked like fun to a naive five-year-old.

Then he saw thirteen-year-old Dee in Philadelphia, listening to the news about Germany's victories in Europe on the radio and understanding just how close he had come to being swept up into the Nazi army. To being D. Kaufmann, dead in a ditch on the wrong side of history at Normandy. Understanding then how his parents had forsaken their homeland, surrendered it to the Nazis without a fight, to save their only child.

And how the United States had saved them all.

It was time to repay those debts.

"I'll take it," Dee said. "I'll blow up the tank."

"What? No!" Sid said, but Dee had already snatched up the satchel.

It was a suicide mission. Sid knew that, and so did Dee. The Germans would gun him down before he ever got close enough to use it. But like picking up the chair in the French house, it felt *right*. Like Dee was restoring balance to the universe.

"Dee, there are other soldiers—soldiers who are already dying," Sid argued.

"They wouldn't make it as far as I would," Dee said. "It's okay," he told Sid, suddenly calm. "I want to do this."

"Wait till after the panzer fires again," the sergeant told Dee.

Dee nodded. He propped the Lucky Soldier's rifle up against the side of the house. He wasn't going to need it. Not where he was going.

Maybe the bullets will just keep missing me, like the Lucky Soldier, Dee thought. Then he remembered how the Lucky Soldier's luck had run out at the last second.

Sid pulled Dee into a hug.

"See you on the other side," Sid told him.

"Nice to know you, buddy," Dee said. "Even if you are a Dodgers fan."

Sid laughed.

Pa-CHOOM!

The tank fired again, and a house collapsed into the street, burying two screaming soldiers.

"Go! Go!" the sergeant cried.

Dee sprinted out into the street. Bullets pinged off the cobblestones at his feet. Dee looked up, and there was the panzer, one block away and larger than life. It was twice as tall as Dee, and six times as wide. Its forward-mounted machine gun spat bullets at him—*chung-chung-chung-chung-chung*—and Dee ducked and ran diagonally.

"Cover fire!" he heard Sid cry.

Behind Dee, the American soldiers who were left stepped out from their hiding places and shot at the second stories of the shops and restaurants down the street. Dee saw the helmet of a German soldier here and there in a window, but the cover fire kept their heads low for the precious few seconds Dee needed to get closer to the tank. His boots slipped on the uneven cobblestones. He stumbled but kept his legs under him. Closer—closer—closer—he just had to get in range to hit the panzer with a good throw.

The tank's treads clanked, and it turned, putting Dee dead in its sights. The forward machine gun erupted again—*chung-chung-chung-chung-chung*. Dee pulled the pin on the grenade. Reared back to throw the satchel at the tank.

Chung-chung-chung-chung-chung.

A bullet struck Dee as he threw the bag, and he spun and fell, hitting the ground the same moment the satchel charge exploded.

REVENGE

KRA-ka-THOOM!

The C-2 exploded a split second after the grenade, booming like a lightning strike in the small village. The blast lifted Dee up and tossed him across the hard cobblestones. He finally came to a rest spread-eagle on the street, sure he had missed the tank with the satchel and even more sure he was dying. His head spun. His eyes blinked stars. Every inch of him hurt. And then—

Pa-CHOOM!

The panzer fired again, the shell ripping the air just above his head. He was right. He hadn't taken out the German tank. He was going to die for nothing.

I'm sorry, Mom, he thought as he cried into the cobblestones. *I'm sorry, Dad.*

"They can't move!" Dee heard the sergeant cry. "Get around behind it, where the armor's weaker!"

His eyes still bleary, his head still swimming, Dee looked up. There was something wrong with the panzer. Its turret still turned and its forward machine gun still fired, but it listed to one side, and a long chain of metal planks spilled out into the street like a broken bicycle chain. *The tank's left tread was gone!* Dee hadn't destroyed the panzer, but he had crippled it. Like *Achilles* back on the beach, the tank could still fire, but it wasn't going anywhere. And what it could hit with its guns was now limited the same way that *Achilles* had been.

As Dee's senses slowly came back to him, he realized *he* might only have taken partial damage as well. He'd been hit in the right arm as he threw the satchel, but he couldn't feel any other serious wounds, and his arms and legs and fingers and toes all moved.

Pakow. Pakow-pakow. Bullets still flew on both sides. No one seemed to be aiming at *him* anymore, but Dee still had to get to cover. He lay in the middle of the street, a few yards away from either sidewalk, and even farther from the protection of any buildings.

The closest cover around was the panzer itself.

Slowly, gingerly, hoping no one would notice, Dee crawled toward the tank. The thing was huge. It was nearly the size of a city bus and probably weighed as much as a herd of elephants. Dee slithered into the open space underneath, between the treads, just as the thing fired again—*pa-CHOOM*. Dee cringed as dust and debris exploded into the street, but he couldn't see if anyone was hurt. If nothing else, he'd prevented the panzer from running them all down. How they were going to stop it from blasting them all with its cannon was another matter entirely.

"Damn it, they're running away down the alleys," someone said, clear as day.

Dee frowned. Who was talking? And where were they? Dee couldn't see any other boots on the street. And there was something strange about the words themselves.

Dee realized what it was with a start. He was so surprised he banged his head against armored panzer above him.

The person was speaking German. Dee could hear the Nazi soldiers in the tank!

"We have to go after them," another Nazi soldier said.

"Well, I *can't* go after them. That pig dog blew off my tread because *you* couldn't hit him with the machine gun!"

"Maybe if you knew how to *steer*—"

"Be quiet," a stern voice told them. "Radio the lieutenant. Tell him to set the church on fire and retreat. We'll regroup with the 21st Panzer Division near Bayeux."

"Yes, Captain," a soldier said. The other soldiers in the tank were quiet as the radio man relayed the orders.

Dee blinked. *Set the church on fire? Why would they want to do that?* he wondered. *Just to cover their retreat?* The American army wouldn't stop to put out the fire. Not when they had the Germans on the run.

Dee wormed his way around to look at the church. He was much closer to it than when he'd first looked at it from down the street, and though it was getting on toward nightfall, he could see that the windows were boarded up and the door barred. What was inside the church that the Nazis wanted to burn before they ran away? What were they trying to hide?

"Lieutenant Weber acknowledges, Captain," the radio man inside the tank said. "They're setting the church on fire now."

There was a *whoosh* as an incendiary device ignited outside the church, and quickly the whole base of the building was engulfed in flames. The Nazis must have doused the outside of it with gas or kerosene to make it burn so fast.

"Well, at least we'll have our revenge on these Frogs for blowing up the supply depot last month," said one of the men inside the tank.

Frogs? Dee knew what that meant. That was an insulting word other countries used to describe the French. Revenge against *what* French people?

Dee felt the air go out of him as he understood. *The French people from the village.* All the empty houses, the meals left uneaten. The Nazis had dragged them from their homes and boarded them up in the church, and now they were setting fire to it.

Orange flames climbed the church, and black smoke poured out from the cracks in the windows.

Dee had to get out from under the tank. He had to let the others know. He had to get those people out of that building before everyone inside was burned alive!

Dee wiggled to the front of the tank. He had just gotten to his knees and was ready to crawl out and run for the nearest alley when—*tink-tink-tink*—an American grenade came rattling across the cobblestones toward the tank and rolled to a stop right beside him.

FWOOSH

Dee dropped to the ground and turned away from the grenade, curling himself into a ball—there was no time to do anything else.

Fwoosh!

Fwoosh? Dee had been braced for a *bang*, not a *fwoosh*. White smoke suddenly surrounded him. He coughed and choked, and his eyes watered. He was in pain, but he was relieved too—it wasn't a frag grenade, it was a smoke grenade!

Hands grabbed him and dragged him away from the tank. Over the bumpy cobblestones, across the rough concrete of the sidewalk, and finally to a stop behind the corner of a building, out of sight of the tank's turret. Dee hacked and spat, but through his blurry eyes he could see Sid's big face, beaming down at him.

"Gotcha!" Sid said.

Dee put his hands on Sid's arms and nodded his thanks, still unable to talk.

"When you're all right, we'll see if we can't get inside that tank, kill us some Germans at last!" Sid said.

Dee shook his head. He tried to talk but could only cough. Finally, he was able to croak out words.

"No. Sid—we have to get to that—church. There are—people inside."

Sid looked over his shoulder in horror. "What? That place is lit up like a furnace."

"It's—the villagers. That's where they went. They're boarded up—inside."

"That's nuts! How do you know?" asked Sid.

Dee's nose and throat still burned, but the tears had stopped. He wiped his eyes with his sleeve.

"I heard—I heard the German soldiers in the tank," Dee said. "When I was underneath."

"They were speaking English?" Sid said.

"No," Dee said. He paused. There was no time to be shy about it, and no time to explain. "I understand German," Dee said. "I'm German, Sid. I was born in Germany."

Sid pulled back from Dee and frowned.

"You're—you're a Kraut?" Sid said. The look of

confusion on his face changed to one of disgust. "What are you—?"

Dee pulled himself to his feet. "Sid, we have to get those people out of that church."

They couldn't go back out into the street—the panzer was still there, and some of the German snipers had stayed behind to cover the others' retreat. Dee jogged around the back side of the building instead, coming at the church from a side street. He looked back, expecting Sid to be with him, but he hadn't followed. Dee's heart sank. He knew Sid wouldn't understand. That's why he'd never told him anything. Dee knew how Sid felt about the Germans, and he hadn't wanted this to come between them. But there hadn't been any other way to explain everything to him in time.

Dee ran to one of the tall windows on the side of the church. Flames curled up the side of the building, and the heat made Dee flinch. Inside, he could hear screams. People were still alive!

Dee looked around for something to hit the boards with, but there was nothing. He kicked at them instead. Fire licked at his trousers and shoes, and heat scorched his face. He kicked harder. The boards wobbled but didn't break. Inside, the yelling got louder. The villagers had heard him pounding on the boards, and they were hitting them back, trying to help break through.

"Dee!" Sid cried, his voice full of anger and hate.

Dee turned.

Sid stood a few steps behind him, his rifle aimed right at Dee's head.

DARKNESS

Dee threw up his hands. "Sid, wait—I can explain!"

Pakow!

Dee flinched, but the bullet didn't hit him. He turned. Sid had shot the boards near the top of the window. Sid held his aim for a moment longer, never once looking at Dee. Dee ducked out of the way, realizing Sid was giving the villagers inside time to get away from the window. Seconds later he fired again, and again, and again. With each bullet the wood shattered and chipped, weakening the boards. After Sid expended a full clip into the barricade, Dee stepped back in and kicked at the boards.

Crack!

One of the boards broke! Dee kicked again and again, smashing through the wood where Sid's bullets had loosened things up. Someone started bashing the boards from the inside too, and soon Dee could see into the sanctuary.

It was an inferno. Pews burned, and flaming timbers fell from the ceiling. Huddled in the few places that weren't ablaze were groups of women and wailing children. There weren't any men, Dee realized. He didn't want to think what the Nazis had done with the village's men.

Pakow!

Bits of rock kicked off the stonework around the window, and Dee flinched again, thinking Sid had shot at him. But it wasn't Sid. A German sniper up in a second-story window somewhere in the village had spotted them and was trying to stop them from getting the prisoners out of the church. Without a word, Sid slapped a new clip in his rifle and returned fire, covering Dee.

Dee kicked and pulled at what was left of the boards. The hot, charred wood scorched his hands, but he wasn't going to stop. At last he made room for the first child to be handed out, and he took a little girl from her mother and set her on the ground outside. Another bullet pinged off the wall of the church, and Sid shifted his aim to fire back.

"Behind the café!" Dee told the girl, pointing the way to cover, and off she ran.

Dee lifted more children across the sill, then he

helped pull a woman through, and she stayed with him to help people out, doubling his speed. Another woman came through and went to watch the children who had already been rescued. Dee and his helper pulled more and more children through the flames as Sid's rifle blazed.

Pa-KOOM. They all ducked, even Sid, as an explosion boomed from out in the street. The panzer had been hit with another explosive from behind, where its armor was weakest, and one of the German soldiers inside was waving a white flag. The sniper bullets stopped too, and Sid turned to help pull women from the fire. More soldiers joined them now that the fighting was done, and they pulled the remaining women through the window as the flaming roof came crashing down inside.

They had saved every last one of the women and children trapped in the church.

"Sid—we did it!" Dee said. "We got them all out!"

Sid heard him, but he didn't turn around. He wouldn't look at him.

Dee sagged. Sid had been his best friend in the army. His best friend ever. But Sid hated Germans, and Dee understood why. It couldn't have helped that he'd lied to Sid all this time. Dee wished now he'd never told Sid the truth, but the damage was done.

The remaining GIs gathered in the small town

square, between the burning church and the now-burning panzer tank. With them, at gunpoint, were the German prisoners they had taken from the tank. The sun was finally down now, and the only light was the hellish orange glow of the destruction both sides had wrought.

The sergeant who'd put together the satchel charge was there, and he clapped Dee on the shoulder. "Good work stopping that tank and rescuing those women and children," he said. "The rest of the Germans retreated," he told them all. "We need to press on after them, toward Bayeux. We'll get one of the locals to give us directions. In the meantime, I need one soldier to stay behind to watch the prisoners until more GIs come through off the beaches."

"I'll guard them," Sid volunteered.

"I'll stay with you," said Dee.

"He said he only needed *one* soldier to watch them," Sid said. He was talking to Dee, but he still wouldn't look at him.

Dee nodded sadly. So this was it. This was where he and Sid parted ways, never to see each other again. Driven apart by who Dee was, and where he'd been born.

Dee reached out for Sid to say goodbye but stopped short. Sid had made it clear he didn't want to think about Dee ever again. The other soldiers moved off down the street, and Dee left Sid with the prisoners and went to collect another discarded rifle.

"You like setting churches on fire with women and children inside, do you?" Dee heard Sid bark at the German prisoners. "Same way you like rounding up Jews and sending them to concentration camps?" They couldn't understand his words, of course, but they understood his anger well enough. The Germans watched Sid warily and kept their hands up.

Sid slapped a fresh cartridge into his rifle.

"Why don't you all just line up against that wall over there," Sid told them. He waved his rifle toward the alley, and fear dawned on the Germans' faces as they comprehended what Sid meant.

Dee understood too. When the rest of the Americans were gone, Sid was going to line the Nazis up and shoot them.

"Sid, don't," Dee said.

"Go. Go!" Sid ordered the Nazis, ignoring Dee.

"Sid, you can't kill them in cold blood. It's murder."

Sid swung around, his face screwed up in anger. He held his rifle waist-high, aimed now at Dee.

"Oh, defending your countrymen, are you?" Sid said. "Now we see your true colors."

"They're not my countrymen anymore," Dee told him. He wanted to explain, to tell Sid about his uncle Otto, about the Night and Fog, how they had come to the United States. Why he had joined the army. But not like this. Not here, not now, in the middle of a French village in Normandy between a burning church and a burning tank. Not with five Nazi soldiers for an audience.

"I don't care about these men," Dee said. "I wish they were dead for what they did. But they're prisoners now, Sid, not soldiers. You can't just execute them."

One of the Nazi soldiers had been watching their back and forth, and understood that Dee was arguing in their favor. "Tell him not to shoot us!" the Nazi said in German. There was no way he could know that Dee could understand him, but he was desperate. "Tell him we were just taking orders!" the Nazi begged.

All the pent-up fury of surviving Omaha and getting shot at and losing Sid erupted out of Dee, and he turned on the Nazi with such a roar that the prisoners stepped back, even though Dee was half a head shorter than any of them.

"You don't deserve his mercy!" Dee cried. *"Just following orders?* What kind of person follows orders to kill innocent women and children? What kind of person does anything that madman Hitler tells you to do?"

Chik-chik.

The sound made Dee turn. Sid had cocked his rifle and was aiming it right at him. Dee slumped. Sid had just heard him yell at the Nazis in German. It didn't matter what he'd said—just hearing the German language come out of Dee's mouth like a native speaker was enough to ruin whatever chance Dee had to salvage their friendship.

Dee raised his hands in surrender.

"Don't shoot them, Sid. Then you'll be just as bad as they are."

Sid looked Dee straight in the eyes. "Get out of here, Dee," he said, his voice cold. "Get out of here, or I'll shoot you too."

Dee held Sid's gaze for a long moment, hoping his friend would see reason. But there was nothing in Sid's eyes but fury.

Dee turned around and walked away.

He was on his own now. It was "Dee-Day" after all. *His* day, and his alone. And all by himself he would march on to Bayeux, and then Paris, and then on to Berlin, the city of his birth.

Halfway through a field outside of town, Dee heard rifle shots behind him. One. Two. Three. Four. Five.

Dee took a deep breath and kept moving.

He didn't need anyone else with him to defeat Hitler. He had a rifle, and ammunition, and no other purpose in life than this. He would march on and do what he had joined the army to do in the first place: give his life to stop the Nazis.

Thwack.

A bullet caught Dee square in the shoulder, knocking him back. He dropped his rifle as he fell, and his helmet went flying. Darkness engulfed him, and he was unconscious before he hit the ground.

OPERATION
BATHING SUIT

JUNE 6, 1944

NIGHT

OMAHA BEACH

I WILL WAIT

Darkness engulfed Monique Marchand inside the small beach hut. She didn't have a watch, but she figured it must be well after eight o'clock at night.

It had also, more importantly, been at least half an hour since Monique heard the last gunshot or explosion on this part of the beach.

Monique's stomach growled, and she shivered as the cool night air cut through the gaps in the wooden shack. She had been inside this hut since eight o'clock this morning—twelve hours! Her mother was used to her being out and about all day, riding her bicycle along the shore or swimming, and she wouldn't miss her. Not until curfew. But from the sounds of things outside, there might not be a German curfew anymore.

Or any *Germans*, for that matter.

But Monique wouldn't know until she left the beach hut. Or at least peeked outside.

Whatever had happened here today, Monique shouldn't have been there. Some places in the sea and on the beach were free of mines, and you could still go swimming. Monique had done just that yesterday, but she had accidentally left her bathing suit in the hut here on the beach after she'd changed, and she had biked back to get it this morning.

And arrived at the exact same moment the war had come to Normandy, France.

She'd been hiding here ever since, curled up in the sand at the bottom of the hut, her arms over her head, singing loud enough to drown out the explosions.

Almost loud enough.

Monique sang when she got nervous. She caught herself now singing Rina Ketty's "J'attrendai." She smiled at that. *J'attrendai* meant "I Will Wait." That could have been her theme song. Hiding curled up at the bottom of a beach hut while things happened outside was the story of her life in a nutshell. She was always afraid to jump in, to make a splash. Take risks. Even now, she wanted to wait. Wanted to hide out in this hut forever—or at least until the sound of engines and shouting soldiers was gone. But life was happening out there. Happening without her. If she didn't leave now, she never would.

Her stomach in a knot, Monique stood up, opened the door a few centimeters, and peeked outside.

It was dark, but her eyes had long since adjusted to the night. She usually knew this stretch of beach like the back of her hand—she had lived every day of her thirteen years in the little village right up the road, after all—but the once-familiar landscape now looked like nothing she'd ever seen before.

The water, just beyond the shore, was filled with lights like stars. But not stars. They were the lights from ships. Dozens of them. Hundreds. As far as she could see. Smaller boats that rode up onto the sand, delivering trucks and tanks and men who carried their own lights, and larger ships, farther off, that roamed the sea like dark leviathans.

The invasion. Monique knew that's what this must be—the much-expected, oft-discussed Allied invasion of France. "I Will Wait" was so popular because that's all any of them had been doing since the Nazis conquered France in 1940. Waiting for someone to come and save them. And now they had finally done it! But *here*? In her backyard? Monique had never expected that! The Germans had built their defenses up and down the Atlantic—the "Iron Coast," they called it on the radio—from the south of France all the way up to Denmark. Forts and bunkers for thousands and thousands of miles. And the Allies had picked her little part of Normandy to invade?

Away from the trucks and men—soldiers, Monique corrected herself—the beach was different too. Before, it had been smooth sand interrupted only by the big X-shaped metal obstacles the Nazis had placed there. Now most of the obstacles remained, but the smooth sand was dotted with craters big and small. Abandoned gear and weapons of all kinds littered the beach, and olive-green lumps dotted the waterline.

Bodies, Monique realized. She put a hand to her mouth and gasped. All those olive-green lumps were soldiers. She had heard the battle raging from where she hid in the bathing hut, and it had sounded terrible. But she'd had no idea of the human cost.

Most of the soldiers were dead, but Monique could see some who still moved, still called out for help. There were medics on the beach—she could tell who they were from their white armbands with the red crosses on them—but there weren't nearly enough to take care of all the wounded.

One of the bodies a few meters away groaned something that sounded like the French word for *doctor*, but nobody heard him.

Nobody but Monique.

She looked up the beach, past the smoldering grass on the dunes. Was her bike still up there, or had it been destroyed in the constant shelling from the ships? Monique wanted to go look for it. Bike straight home. Crawl back into the beach hut of her quiet life with her mother, and shut the door.

But then there was the soldier lying in the sand, moaning, "Medic. Medic."

It was time to leave the hut.

Singing "I Will Wait" to herself, Monique tiptoed toward the soldier.

BONJOUR

Monique looked around anxiously, worried someone would see her going onto the battlefield instead of away from it.

Monique was tall for her thirteen years, and on the thin side—just like everyone else who had suffered through four years of food shortages during the Nazi occupation. But there was no way that anyone would mistake her for a soldier. Her brown hair was down to her shoulders, and she wore a simple, short-sleeved blue denim dress that buttoned down the front and was belted at the waist. Her slightly oversized green rubber boots were the only good pair of shoes she owned anymore—and the laughingstock of the neighborhood—but they proved useful now in keeping her feet out of the wet sand.

And the blood.

Monique knew she wasn't supposed to be there, but all the soldiers swarming the beach had other things to worry about, and she made it to the injured man without being noticed at all. Some of the kids Monique knew from school were squeamish around anything to do with blood or guts, but Monique never had been. Once, when a boy had dislocated his fingers after a hard fall in a soccer game in the street, Monique had surprised everyone—herself included—when she had been the only one who would pull them back into place again. (One of the other boys who'd been watching had fainted when she'd done it.) From that point on, Monique had been known as "Dr. Monique" in the schoolyard. Even if it had been meant as a joke, it had given her the idea to read up on first aid in the public library.

Before the Nazis had closed it and burned all the books.

Monique knelt down nervously by the wounded soldier. She wasn't afraid of what she might see—that's partially what had brought her over in the first place. She was worried she would get in trouble for being there.

The soldier lay on his side, and Monique peered at him. He wasn't German. She knew what those uniforms looked like. And he wasn't French—there wasn't a French army anymore. Not to speak of. She'd heard rumors of a Resistance but had never seen them. This soldier was one of the Allies, then, she was sure. But British? American? *American*, she thought. Weren't they the ones who wore green in the propaganda posters?

What she *could* tell was that the soldier was injured in two places: a lighter bullet wound in his left arm and something more serious in his right leg.

Monique looked around anxiously, but still no one noticed her.

If no one else is going to help him, then I am, Monique decided.

Humming "I Will Wait," Monique stopped waiting and tore the man's trousers away from the bloody wound on his leg. A bullet had gone right through his thigh, shattering his femur. Monique's eyes went wide. She could see the broken bone in the wound. *Fascinating*. She had only seen pictures of bones in books!

The soldier's skin was ashen and cool to the touch, but when she put a finger to the pulse in his arm, she felt his heart racing. This was something called shock. The man's heart was overcompensating for his loss of blood. How long had he been lying like this? Why weren't there more medics?

Monique didn't know if his leg could be saved, but this man would be dead long before that if she couldn't stop the bleeding. Using the soldier's belt and the handle of his collapsible shovel, she fashioned a serviceable tourniquet, stanching the flow of blood from the wound.

As she worked, Monique sang, which seemed to calm the soldier down. His shoulders relaxed, and the painful frown left his face. Monique suddenly worried he wasn't relaxed at all but was slipping into unconsciousness—or worse, dying—and she stopped.

The soldier's eyes opened at once, and though he didn't seem to see Monique, he spoke to her. He said something in English Monique didn't understand, but one word came through loud and clear: "Mama."

Monique blushed. The soldier must have been confusing her singing with his mother singing to him when he was a boy. When he was a *younger* boy. He couldn't have been a year out of high school himself. She felt awkward, this young man calling her "Mama." But what he needed right now was comfort.

Monique sang to him again, haltingly this time, still embarrassed, and he closed his eyes again and relaxed.

Monique tore material from his ripped trousers to make a bandage for his arm, and tied it off.

Yes. Good, Monique thought. She let out a deep breath. The man needed much more help than she could provide, but she'd done something, and no one had caught her and sent her away.

Then someone behind her said, *"Bonjour,"* and Monique jumped out of her skin.

BUSTED

Monique spun around. An American medic with a canvas stretcher was standing right behind her! Monique immediately bowed her head.

"I'm sorry," she said in French. "I know I shouldn't be here. It's just, I came to the beach today to collect my bathing suit, and then there was the invasion, and so many soldiers need help—"

The medic knelt to examine the soldier. "This is good work," she said in French.

She. Monique looked up at the medic in surprise. "You're—you're a woman! A woman doctor!" she cried.

The woman smiled. She had pale skin and a round, kind face, with curly brown flyaway hair tucked up under her green helmet. "I'm not, really," she said. "I mean, yes, I am a woman. But I'm not a doctor or medic of any kind. I'm a reporter. I just dressed up as a medic to get on the beach. They wouldn't let me be here other-wise." She held a finger to her lips. "I won't tell on you if you don't tell on me. The name's Dorothy. Dorothy Powell."

Monique introduced herself, and they shook hands.

Dorothy looked at the soldier again. "You may have saved his life," she told Monique. "Let's get him to the medical tent."

Monique's chest swelled with pride, but just as quickly she was panicking again.

"The medical tent? But if they catch me here—"

"No one's paying any attention," Dorothy said. "But here." She picked up the soldier's helmet and put it on Monique's head, tucking Monique's hair up under it. The helmet was heavy and floppy and way too big for her, but it certainly hid her. "He's not going to need it anymore, that's for sure. Now help me get him on this stretcher."

Together, Monique and Dorothy unrolled the can-vas stretcher and lifted the now-sleeping soldier onto it carefully, gently.

"One, two, three, *lift*," Dorothy said, and they stag-gered off through the sand toward a tent a few dozen meters away.

"You're a reporter?" Monique asked the woman as they went.

Dorothy nodded. "With *Collier's*, in America. They

sent me to cover the war, but the army disapproves of women reporters in active fighting situations. Not men reporters, mind you. Ernie Pyle can go war-horsing all over North Africa and Italy with soldiers, but we women are stuck well behind the lines doing puff pieces. So I snuck aboard a medical ship in England, stole a uniform, and came ashore with the relief corps."

Monique couldn't believe it. The daring of it—to stow away, to disguise herself, to come ashore while there was still danger.

"If you're a reporter, why are you helping take care of soldiers?" Monique asked.

Dorothy's smile faded. "I admit, I came here just to observe. To report. But no one who saw what happened here today could just stand by and watch, could they? *You* couldn't." She paused as they negotiated a tricky crater. "All these poor men," Dorothy said at last. "Not even men. Boys, most of them. They look like they could be in high school. I dare say many of them still would be if there hadn't been a war. It's America's future we're sacrificing here on these beaches, and in Africa, and Italy, and the Pacific, and the skies over Germany."

Monique nodded. The Nazis had also stolen France's future—and their present too. How many men and women had she seen taken from her village? How many boys and girls? There was almost no one left. Monique's two much younger sisters had been sent to stay with their aunt in the city of Lyon, where it was safer, while Monique stayed in Normandy with her mother. Monique's father was gone too—sent to work in a factory in Germany. Hope and fear tugged at Monique's heart—would she ever see her dad alive again? Would the invasion mean he was finally free to come home? Her sisters too? It seemed like forever since they had all been together as a family.

Dorothy and Monique arrived at the medical tent, where dozens of medics and soldiers were moving here and there in what amounted to barely controlled chaos. Monique kept her head down and tried not to make eye contact with anyone.

"Got another one for you," Dorothy called.

Monique's heart jumped into her throat. Dorothy was disguised in a uniform, but even though Monique wore a helmet, she was still wearing her dress and rubber boots. She stood out like—like a French girl in the middle of an American military base. What if they were angry at her? What if they threw her into some sort of military jail?

What if they told her mother?

Two soldiers came up to take the stretcher away from them, and Monique looked at the ground and held her breath.

To her great surprise, neither of the soldiers said a word. They were too busy to worry about who brought the stretcher to them, and they took the wounded man away without even acknowledging Dorothy and Monique.

"What did I tell you?" Dorothy whispered.

Dorothy snatched scissors and tape and bandages from a cart and thrust them at Monique.

Monique hesitated. She was worried someone would see, yes. But what really gave her pause was her own fear. Could she do this? *Should* she do this? What if she tried to help someone, and did more harm than good?

What if she failed?

"Come on, Monique. Take them," Dorothy said. She offered the medical supplies again with a quick look around to make sure no one was watching.

Hiding out in the beach hut is easy, Monique reminded herself. *But life is happening outside.*

Borrowing some of Dorothy's daring, Monique took the pieces of medical equipment and stuffed them in her big pockets. Her heart fluttered.

Dorothy grabbed an empty stretcher, and together they ran back out to look for more wounded soldiers.

Back and forth they went, all evening, bandaging up soldiers as best they could and bringing them back to the medical tent. Monique quickly forgot the cold and her hunger. She didn't have time for either one.

From the medical tent, some of the wounded were sent on by truck to Bayeux, where there was a hospital.

Those were the soldiers who might recover and be sent back to the front. Most of the others—like the man Monique found propped up against one of the big metal obstacles with a syringe tube stuck in his chest to drain air from a chest cavity wound—were put back on Higgins boats to ferry them out to the big white medical ships that floated like ghosts just off the coast. Once the medical ships were full, Dorothy explained, the wounded soldiers would be carried away to England and the proper hospitals there, before being sent back home.

The rest were put in body bags.

Dorothy and Monique worked until their hands got blisters. The blisters tore and oozed and stung on the wooden stretcher handles, but Monique wrapped them in bandages so they could keep working.

"What's that song you're singing?" Dorothy asked her.

Monique blushed. She hadn't realized she was singing out loud again.

"'I Will Wait,'" Monique said.

"What's it about?" Dorothy asked.

"A girl, she says she will wait forever, night and day, until the man she loves comes back to her," Monique explained. "It's a very popular song here in France."

"That would be a popular song just about anywhere in the world right now," Dorothy said, her eyes taking in all the young men who lay dead on the beach. Monique understood what she meant. There would be a lot of young women waiting forever for young men who would never return.

Monique knelt to wrap the arm of another wounded soldier who would return, just not, perhaps, in one piece.

"You're pretty handy with a bandage," Dorothy said.

"I want to be a nurse," Monique said.

"I've seen your work, my dear, and you have no business being a nurse," Dorothy said.

Monique looked away, hurt, until Dorothy lowered her kind, round face into Monique's line of vision and smiled. "You shouldn't be a nurse, my dear. You should be a doctor."

Monique beamed, and hope filled her. *A woman doctor? Who'd ever heard of such a thing?* she thought. But why not? She could do the job just as well as any man. Better.

The rest of the night, Monique was half in the present here on the beach and half in the future in a hospital, where she wore a white coat and attended patients as a surgeon. Along the way, Dorothy picked up pieces of "I Will Wait," and they sang it together as they worked.

Sometime later, back in the medical tent for the umpteenth time, Dorothy bent over too sluggishly to pick up another stretcher, and her helmet slipped off. Her frizzy hair fluffed out like popcorn bursting from a kernel. She stood quickly, trying to smooth it down, to pull it down in the back with her fist, but the jig was up. Half the soldiers in the tent had seen it happen and were gaping at them.

Dorothy and Monique were busted.

THE PRETTIEST TOILET YOU EVER SAW

"You there! Who are you? You can't be here!" the beach master cried, charging up to Dorothy. He spoke French, but with a strange, flat accent. He was a stout man with a red face and a black mustache like a walrus, and his job was to coordinate all the many moving pieces on this part of the beach post-invasion. And those pieces, apparently, did not include a woman reporter and an amateur nurse. "And you, young lady!" he said to Monique. "What the devil are *you* doing here?"

Monique's first instinct was to look away, to beg forgiveness. But she was tired of lying low, tired of not speaking up or speaking out. She had picked up a little of Dorothy's stubbornness too. Besides, it was time to call a cat a cat: She had *helped*, really helped, and she knew it. What right did this man have to tell her she couldn't be on this beach? It was *her* beach, after all, not his.

Monique held her head high. "I've been bandaging soldiers and moving them into the tent," she said.

"That's not what I mean!" the beach master said. "You're neither one allowed here."

"And why not?" Dorothy asked.

"Because it's not safe!" the beach master told her.

"It's not safe for you either," said Dorothy. "But here you are."

"Because I'm a—"

"Man?" Dorothy finished for him.

The beach master looked flustered. "Yes," he said. "And a soldier. It's my *job* to be here."

"Mine too," Dorothy told him. "I'm a reporter with *Collier's*."

"And I live here," said Monique.

The beach master scowled at them. "Nobody who can't dig a latrine should be allowed in battle," he said, as though that settled it.

Dorothy put out her blistered, bandaged hand. "If you'll give me a shovel, Captain, I'll dig you the prettiest toilet you ever saw. Good enough for your crap, anyway."

Monique's eyes went wide, and she put a hand to her open mouth. One of the soldiers who'd been carrying stretchers back and forth all night alongside them snickered, and the beach master looked affronted.

"No? Then can we please get back to moving these boys off the beach?" Dorothy asked wearily.

"They been working real hard, sir," the other stretcher-bearer said. "Just as hard as the rest of us. And we could use all the hands we can get."

When Dorothy translated what he'd said, Monique was surprised. She thought no one had taken any notice of them, but clearly someone had.

"You'll leave my beach this instant," the beach master told Dorothy and Monique, "or I'll have you arrested and hauled away."

Dorothy held up her hands in surrender. "Have it your way, Captain. Come along, Monique."

Monique couldn't believe Dorothy would give up so easily, and she followed along dejectedly. It had felt so incredible to be useful, to be contributing something to the invasion that was here to free her country from Nazi rule. Even though it had been tiring, painful, emotionally difficult work, Monique would have kept doing it until the last man was taken care of if she could.

When they were outside the tent, out of the view of the beach master, Dorothy took Monique's hand and pulled her behind one of the trucks being loaded up with patients bound for Bayeux.

"Forget that pompous fool," Dorothy whispered. "How would you like to hitch a ride to Bayeux and see a real military hospital in action?"

WARNING: MINES

"Bayeux's not far from here, is it?" Dorothy said. She hitched a foot up on the bumper of a truck and grabbed the side. "We can be there and back before it gets late."

"What? No. But—" Monique stammered. She had found the courage to leave the beach hut, to join Dorothy in helping wounded soldiers, to stand up to the beach master. But to leave her village and go to Bayeux?

Dorothy hopped up into the back of the truck. It was meant to have a canvas roof over the back end, but since it wasn't raining, the truck drivers had taken it off so the wounded could be loaded and unloaded more quickly.

Dorothy found a place to kneel among the stretchers and put a hand out to Monique. "Come on!" she said. "More medics have arrived here on the beach anyway.

They've got things under control. Let's see what we can do to help elsewhere."

"I Will Wait" popped into Monique's head again, and she felt the pull of her own fear. She bit a fingernail. This was too much, surely. It was so much easier to say no, to find her bike in the grass and go home.

And hide, she scolded herself. If she was going to do that, she might as well go crawl back in the beach hut. No—she had stepped out into the Allied invasion, and she wasn't going back.

Monique took Dorothy's hand and pulled herself up. The truck began to move, and Monique settled in beside one of the wounded soldiers.

"Oh!" Monique said, suddenly remembering. *The hut.* "I left my bathing suit in the changing hut again!"

"What do you mean?" Dorothy asked.

Monique told Dorothy the story of why she'd gone to the beach that morning in the first place, and the reporter laughed.

"Well, you can rest assured your bathing suit is now being protected by thousands of strapping young American men, my dear," Dorothy told her.

Monique blushed and looked away, over the fields that stretched out from the dunes beyond the town.

"Wait! Stop the truck! Stop the truck!" Monique cried.

Dorothy grabbed her arm in alarm. "What is it?" she asked.

"A wounded soldier, there in the field." Monique stood and pointed. "I can see him breathing. It looks bad, but no one's gone to help him."

"Stop the truck!" Dorothy called out in English to the driver.

"What? Why?" the soldier called back. "Wait, are you a dame?"

"Oh, dash it all, there will be other trucks," Dorothy told Monique. "Come on."

"What are you—?" Monique began, but Dorothy was already climbing out of the truck. While it was moving! Monique hurried to follow her. No time to debate it now; Monique didn't want to get separated from Dorothy. Together they climbed down to the bottom step at the back of the truck, and on the count of three, they jumped onto the dirt road. They both fell and tumbled, but Monique was up in a flash and running toward the field.

"Wait!" Dorothy called after her, but Monique kept going. She was done waiting. She ran until she felt Dorothy grab her by the arm and pull her back. "Wait, Monique! That sign—I can read a little German. The important bits, at least. And that sign says 'Warning: Mines' in German. That must be why no one's gone after him." She nodded to the still figure of the soldier up ahead.

"No, no," Monique said. "There are no mines." She tried to pull her arm away from Dorothy.

"Monique, stop! I want to help that boy as much as you do, but that sign says he's stuck in the middle of a minefield! There's nothing we can do until the mine-sweepers make it up off the beach."

"*No*," Monique told her. "You don't understand. It's not a real minefield at all. The Germans, they *meant* to bury mines here, but they never got around to it. I know—I come by here every day! They just put that sign up to trick people. The Germans were playing soccer in that field just yesterday!"

Monique finally pulled herself free and ran for the soldier. Dorothy still called after her, but Monique didn't wait. There were no mines in the field, and she knew it.

When Dorothy saw Monique was right, she followed her into the field.

Monique knelt by the American soldier. He was very young, and short and skinny. He looked like he wasn't even out of school yet. He was cute too, Monique thought, despite the bandage on his arm, the cut on his face, and the bullet wound to his shoulder. He had blond hair, long lashes, and a quiet, restful face.

Dorothy came up behind her. "Another boy," she said. "And this one even younger than the rest."

"He's got minor injuries that have already been treated by someone," Monique said, looking him over, "but he's taken a bullet to the shoulder and has lost a lot of blood." She looked around, surprised he was the only wounded soldier in the whole field. "Where were your friends?" Monique whispered to him. "Why didn't you have anyone with you who could help?"

The boy didn't answer, of course. Even if he understood French, he was long since unconscious.

"Do you still have the bandages?" Monique asked.

Dorothy already had the bandages and tape and scissors ready, and Monique hummed a Lucienne Boyer song, "Speak to Me of Love," as she worked.

"You've changed your tune," Dorothy said.

Monique smiled. So she had.

Dorothy pulled out the soldier's dog tags and read the boy's name.

"D. Carpenter. Well, D., this is your lucky day," Dorothy told the unconscious boy. "Dr. Monique is on the case."

OPERATION NEPTUNE

JUNE 6, 1944

CLOSE TO MIDNIGHT

ON THE ROAD TO BAYEUX

SO FAR TO GO

Dee bumped and swayed as he slowly regained consciousness. He heard the growl of an engine and the grinding of gears. He was in a truck. On his back. His body ached, and his head swam, but it was his shoulder that drew his waking attention. It was strangely numb and sore at the same time. He remembered leaving Sid behind with the prisoners in the village. Gunshots. A field. All by himself, ready to give his life to stop Hitler—

Dee's eyes fluttered open, and he saw stars. Some of them were in his eyes, like he'd just rubbed them, but more of them were tiny twinkling lights in the sky. He was in the back of an army truck with its canvas roof taken off.

D-Day had become D-Night. Had he really just

come ashore in France that morning? It seemed like a lifetime ago.

"It looks like your patient is awake, Doctor," a woman said.

Her face appeared above Dee, a round, kind face that blocked out the stars. Another face joined hers, that of a young girl, and Dee blinked stupidly, his brain still foggy. The girl said something in French, and the woman translated for her.

"Dr. Monique says you may be a bit groggy," she told Dee. "You lost a lot of blood, and you had to be given morphine for the pain."

"Doctor?" Dee said. He didn't understand. "A girl? How old—?"

"Thirteen," the woman said. "And what, you don't think a thirteen-year-old French girl can be a doctor? Look at you. You can't be much older, and you're a soldier."

"I'm—I'm sixteen," Dee said, his muddy head making him honest about his age.

"Boys and girls, playing at war," the woman said quietly.

"Are you—nurses?" Dee asked, still trying to understand.

"I'm a reporter," the woman said. "Dorothy Powell, *Collier's* magazine. And Monique here isn't a nurse, she's a doctor. In training."

Dee was having trouble keeping up. "Where—?" he tried to ask.

"We're on our way to a hospital in Bayeux," Dorothy said.

Dee tried to sit up.

"*Non, non, non, non,*" Dr. Monique said, pushing him back down.

"Now, now," Dorothy said. "You're not going anywhere with that shoulder until we get you some proper treatment."

"And then—back to my platoon," Dee said. "If any of the guys from my platoon are still alive."

"We'll see," Dorothy said.

Monique asked Dorothy a question in French, and Dorothy answered her. Dee didn't understand their conversation, but Monique's expression and tone told him she didn't think he had much chance of returning to the fight. But he would. He would show them. He lay back and closed his eyes. He had to keep fighting. Had to make up for what his former countrymen were doing to the world.

Dee zoned in and out as they bounced along, and as his brain got less muddled, the pain in his shoulder grew. Perhaps the wound was worse than he thought. But it was only a shoulder. He could still run, still pull a trigger.

The road got smoother, and buildings began to appear. They were in Bayeux at last.

Bayeux. Dee suddenly remembered: That was the town the Englishman from the tank had talked about.

Bill. The Bayeux Tapestry. Dee felt a lump in his throat. *Bill is never going to get to Bayeux now, never going to see his tapestry,* Dee thought sadly. Dee would ask around about the tapestry, go see it if he could, before he moved on to the front. For Bill and the *Achilles* crew.

Dee propped himself up on his good side to try to see the city. Now that Bayeux was under Allied control and not worried about British bombers, all the street-lights were on.

The city was, amazingly, still in one piece. Dee knew that other cities in Normandy had been bombed for months by the Allies, but Bayeux had clearly been spared. It looked as though there hadn't been any fighting here today. Its cobblestone streets and white-brick houses, its cathedrals and canals, its flower-lined avenues and little cafés, they were all preserved, like a dream. Like war had never come to France. Like they had never been occupied by the Nazis.

But war *had* come to Bayeux, and Dee and all the other American and English soldiers were the proof. Soldiers filled the streets of the city, marching, strolling, reconnecting with their regiments. There were so many soldiers coming and going that the tanks and supply trucks pushing for the front could barely navigate the streets.

Dee caught himself looking for Sid's familiar face in the crowd, then stopped. Sid wouldn't want Dee to find him anyway.

There were French people in the streets too. The ones who had stayed in Normandy. Old men and women grabbed soldiers as they passed, hugging them and kissing their cheeks. Children offered soldiers wine and bread, and sang songs from upstairs windows. It felt like a party in Bayeux, not like Day One of the battle to free France.

"Where are the Nazis?" Dee asked.

"Ran away," Dorothy said. "From Bayeux, at least. That's what I was told. No doubt regrouping for a counterattack. But word among the soldiers is that to the east, the Brits are holding two bridges, and the Canadians have taken German garrisons. American paratroopers hold the roads in from the west. All of which happened before you ever set foot on the beach. The Resistance has been active in the south as well. They're all keeping the German reinforcements at bay."

Dee nodded. "It won't hold them off forever though," he said.

"No," Dorothy admitted. "But it's given us a toehold, at least. A place to start."

That's just what Sergeant Taylor had told them,

Dee remembered. All the way back on the landing boat before the ramp had dropped. Before the sergeant had died in Dee's arms. Today was meant to be the first step in pushing the Germans all the way back to Berlin— and incredibly, it had worked.

Bits and pieces of conversations in English filtered up to Dee as the truck inched through the crowds.

"Okay, so the Jerries come out of the château and surrender to us, and there's twice as many of them as there are of us," Dee heard a soldier with a Canadian accent say to another soldier. From the truck, Dee couldn't see the soldiers' uniforms, but he could see that they wore helmets with little shreds of fabric tucked into the netting, the way paratroopers did.

"They were mad as hornets," the Canadian paratrooper went on, "but it's not like they could *un*surrender!"

The two soldiers laughed, and Dee grinned. It was just the kind of thing Sid would have said, if that had happened to them.

If Sid was still alive.

And if Sid was still talking to him.

The street grew too crowded for the truck to move, and the driver laid on the horn and cursed. Beside the truck, Dee saw that a French café was open, and the owner was pouring free drinks for the liberating soldiers.

Allied soldiers crowded around him, raising glasses and toasting each other.

"Hey—no darkies served here," Dee heard someone say.

One of the white American soldiers was standing in the way of a black American medic. Dee realized with a start that he knew him—it was Henry, the man who'd saved Sid's life on the beach, the man who had shown such amazing courage.

"Hey, let him have a drink," Dee yelled from the truck. "He saved my buddy's life!"

But another white American soldier came up, and so did another, forming a wall between the black medic and the owner of the café.

"Go find a colored restaurant," a white soldier told Henry.

Dee tried to get up, to climb out of the truck and stand with the medic, but Dr. Monique said, *"Non non non,"* and pushed him back down again.

Dee saw Henry leave the café without a drink. The medic met Dee's gaze. As the truck lurched and moved on, Henry gave Dee an informal salute before turning and disappearing into the crowd.

Dorothy looked from Henry back to Dee. "We've come so far together," Dorothy said, "but we still have so far to go."

The truck didn't have any farther to go though. It pulled to a stop in the town square, and Dee watched as soldiers began unloading the stretchers. He heard someone say that the hospital was already crowded with patients, and they were instead being moved into a triage center in the plaza across from Bayeux's cathedral. Cots and blankets with wounded soldiers crowded the plaza, and nurses and medics moved among the patients, deciding who would move on to the hospital and who could be treated and released.

Two soldiers grabbed Dee's stretcher, but Dee made them wait before they carried him off.

"Thank you," Dee told Dorothy and Monique. "Whoever you are—you saved my life."

Monique blushed. *"Au revoir,"* she told Dee.

Dorothy nodded at him. "You're welcome," she replied. "Now don't waste it." She gave Dee a mock salute. "See you, kid." She and Monique stood up together. "Now we're off to stick our noses in where they're not welcome some more."

The soldiers carried Dee away and deposited him among the other wounded soldiers in the plaza. A medic appeared beside him—a white medic he hadn't seen before—and without warning, he stuck Dee with a needle in his arm.

"Ow! Hey!" Dee said.

The medic connected the needle to an IV, and soon Dee was getting a transfusion of new blood.

"Can I get back to fighting soon?" Dee asked.

"Somebody'll be along to let you know," the medic said, and before Dee could ask anything else, the medic was already off to see to other wounded soldiers.

Dee lay back and stared up at the night sky above the plaza. It was hard to imagine that back home in Philadelphia it was just around six o'clock. His parents would be coming home from work right now, his classmates hanging out at the drugstore soda counter. All of them safe and sound, while Dee was lying here, shot through the shoulder, in a makeshift hospital in a city in France.

"Thank you," Dee heard a girl say to him in a heavy French accent.

Dee sat up, thinking Dr. Monique had come to see him again. Instead, there was a young brown-skinned girl in front of him, wearing a blue kerchief over her black hair. Beside her, holding the girl's hand like she would never let her go, was a beautiful woman in a tan trench coat, with light brown skin, black hair, a heart-shaped face, and a long, angular nose. The girl's face was rounder, her eyes wider and younger, but the resemblance was unmistakable. They had to be mother and daughter.

"Thank you," the girl said again, and handed Dee a white lily from a bunch of them she held in her hand. Dee accepted the flower, feeling confused.

"My daughter thanks you for saving my life," the woman explained, her English also accented, but easier to understand.

"Were you in the church?" Dee said. He didn't remember helping them through the window, and he couldn't imagine ever forgetting either one of them.

"No," the woman said. "I was being held prisoner here in Bayeux."

Dee looked apologetic and tried to hand the lily back. "Oh, I'm sorry," he said. "I think you must have me confused with someone else. I wasn't the one who freed you."

"Not you alone, no," the woman said. "You *all* did, just by coming here." She looked around, gesturing at the soldiers. "You freed me, and thousands of other people in Normandy. And soon you will free all of France. All of Europe."

"I— Well, thank you," Dee said, accepting the lily from the girl. "What's your name?" he asked, then tried again in phrasebook French. "*Comment vous appelez-vous?*"

The girl smiled at his obvious butchering of her language, but she understood.

"Samira," she said. "*Je m'appelle* Samira."

"Thank you, Samira," Dee said.

The girl nodded to him, and Dee watched as she and her mother moved on to deliver a lily to the next soldier in the row. Who were they? Did they live here in Bayeux? What part had they played in this day?

"Not even here a day," someone said beside Dee, "and you're already a hit with the ladies."

Dee turned.

Sid Jacobstein stood over his bed.

ALLIES

"Sid!" Dee said. The joy at seeing his friend again— still alive!—was quickly replaced by apprehensiveness. The last time he had seen Sid, his friend had pointed a rifle at him and told him to get lost. Now his rifle was over his shoulder, and he turned the stem of the white lily in his hand.

Sid looked uncomfortable, like he didn't know whether to stay or go, or what to say. Dee didn't know what to say either.

"I . . . see you met Samira and her mother," Dee said.

"Huh?" said Sid.

"The lily."

"Oh," Sid said. He relaxed now that he had something to talk about. "Yeah, that girl and her mom, they told me I saved their lives. But I didn't."

"They told me we all did," said Dee.

They didn't speak again for a few long seconds, Sid looking at the flower in his hands and Dee looking at the red tube that snaked down to the needle in his arm.

"I—I saw you getting stretchered off that truck," Sid said at last. "How bad is it?"

"I think my career as a Major League pitcher might be over," said Dee.

Sid snickered. "Listen, kid, I saw you pitch for the barracks team back at training camp. You were *never* going pro."

Dee smiled, then nodded toward his wound. "Seriously, I can barely feel it." Which was true—but most likely because of the morphine. "I'll be back out there fighting Nazis in no time."

Sid turned the lily in his hands again. Dee could tell there was something more Sid wanted to say, but he still didn't know how to say it. He sighed and sat down on the edge of Dee's cot, not quite looking at him but not looking away either.

"I couldn't do it," Sid said. "I couldn't shoot them. Those German soldiers you left me with. I wanted to. I had them all lined up and ready, and I couldn't do it."

Dee blinked. "But I heard gunshots," he said. "On the way out of town."

"New GIs came up from the beach. There were still a couple of German snipers that hung back to give us trouble, and the new boys took care of them. But I guess you know all about the snipers. One of them must have caught you before the others took care of him."

Sid paused. He pulled his helmet off his head and ran his fingers through his dark curly hair.

"I had my gun on those Krauts, the ones I was guarding, and I kept thinking about how they had killed so many of our boys. How they had put all those people in that church and set it on fire. I kept thinking about what the Nazis were doing to Jews all over Europe, and how I still hadn't got to pay a single one of them back." Sid took a breath. "And I *wanted* to kill them, Dee. But I kept thinking about what you said. About being as bad as them if I killed them like that, in cold blood. And I kept thinking how you were a better man than all of us, even if you *were* a Kraut. Sorry—a German. And that there had to be some reason you were on our side, and not theirs . . ."

Dee told Sid his story then. His whole story. How he was Dietrich, not Douglas. Why he and his family had left Germany, and why Dee had wanted to come back, as a US soldier. How if Dee had stayed in Germany, he would have been taught to hate Sid. And how coming to America had meant they became friends instead.

"So, I'm supposed to call you *Dee-trick* now?" Sid said, butchering the pronunciation.

"Just Dee. I was Dee before, and I'm still Dee now."

"And you're not even an American citizen?" Sid asked. He leaned close, conspiratorially. "Does Uncle Sam know?"

Dee laughed. "Yeah. They still let you fight. All you gotta do is hate the Nazis, which is something we both have in common. And I'm going to become one too. An American citizen, that is, not a Nazi! Just as soon as I get home. I've decided. Those Nazis back there, they were never my countrymen. You are."

Sid put his hand out, and Dee took it.

A doctor finally came to examine Dee. He read the chart the first medic had left and peeled back the bandage on Dee's shoulder.

"When can I get back in the fight, Doc?" Dee asked.

The doctor made a notation on Dee's chart and hung it back on his cot. "You're done, son," he said.

Panic welled up inside Dee. "'*Done*'? What do you mean 'done'?"

"I mean you get a Purple Heart and a story to tell the grandkids about how you survived Omaha Beach. Your war is over, kid."

"No—no!" Dee said, but the doctor was already off to see his next patient.

Dee clutched at Sid's arm. "You gotta get him back here. Tell him I'm okay to fight."

Dee winced from the pain in his shoulder, and he fell back on his cot.

"Don't sweat it, Dee," Sid said. "You heard the man. You got a golden ticket back to England for R & R and then back to the States. Which is a lot more than a lot of guys today get to say."

"I know. But you don't understand," Dee said. The weight of everyone he'd seen die today pressed down on him. Their sergeant. Bill and his tank crew. The Lucky Soldier. All the thousands of other men who'd never made it off Omaha Beach. "It's our fault things got this bad," Dee said. "My family's and mine. And I've got to fix it."

"Dee, you did your part. *More* than your part. It's time to go home."

Dee fought back his tears. He didn't want it to end this way. There was more he had to do. More he *could* do to make things right. He'd only spent a single day—D-Day—in the war. He didn't want to go home yet.

"But who's going to liberate Europe?" Dee said. "Who's going to stop the Nazis?"

"Are you nuts?" Sid said with a laugh. "Dee, look around you. You see all these soldiers? You hear all these different languages? All these people from different countries? That's what they're all here for."

Dee dried his eyes and looked around. Sid was right. Dee had never seen so many people come together for a single cause like this. Yes, he'd *seen* them before: on the ships at sea and on the Higgins boats, on the beaches and in the towns of Normandy, on the streets of Bayeux. But he'd been so wrapped up in his own reason for being here, his own reason for fighting the Nazis, that he hadn't thought too long about anyone else.

Now Dee *really* saw them. The medics and the sailors and the pilots and all the soldiers. The paratroopers and Resistance fighters and spies. He thought of all the people back home working in factories, making sacrifices. The entire free world, united for the common good. It was just like Samira and her mother had said— no one of the soldiers had saved them. They *all* had. And now they were going to save the rest of the world.

They were stronger together.

They were allies.

"Don't worry, pal," said Sid. "We got this."

AUTHOR'S NOTE

The Allied invasion of Normandy on June 6, 1944—commonly referred to as D-Day—was, and still is, the largest seaborne invasion in history. Planning for the complicated, international mission began a year ahead of time, led principally by President Franklin D. Roosevelt of the United States and Prime Minister Winston Churchill of the United Kingdom, and their highest-ranking generals.

Shortly after midnight on June 6, nearly 25,000 American, British, and Canadian paratroopers were dropped from planes over Normandy. Their efforts corresponded with countless smaller acts of sabotage and assault carried out by the thousands of French Resistance fighters scattered throughout northern France.

The paratroopers were followed, at dawn, by more than 5,000 Allied ships and landing crafts carrying almost 160,000 soldiers from at least eight different countries. The Allies landed on a fifty-mile stretch of Normandy beach divided by the invasion planners into five zones, each with its own code name: Gold, Juno, and Sword to the east, which were the responsibility of British and Canadian troops, and Omaha and Utah to the west, which were the responsibility of the United States.

Accurate figures are hard to come by, but by the end of the day on June 6, 1944, an estimated 4,500 Allied soldiers would be dead, and more than 10,000 would be wounded—a majority of them American. In the first twenty-four hours of the invasion, more than 3,000 French civilians died in the fighting and bombing, and German losses for the day ranged anywhere between 4,000–9,000 dead.

What is more certain is that, though costly, D-Day was a tremendous victory for the Allies. Once the beaches were secure, the armies of the United States and the United Kingdom poured through into France, pushing the Nazi army back toward Germany. By the end of that August, Paris had been liberated, and the Allies—led by the United States and the United Kingdom in the west, and the Soviet Union in the east—stood on Germany's doorstep. By May of the following year—less than a year after their triumph at D-Day—the Allies had accepted Nazi Germany's unconditional surrender.

June 6, 1944—D-Day—was the beginning of the end of the Second World War.

A NOTE ON OPERATION NAMES

The entire plan for D-Day was code-named Operation Overlord, but there were dozens—if not hundreds—of smaller operations and missions, each with their own separate code names that fell under the larger Overlord umbrella. The names were often nonsensical, to hide what they were really about, though some seem rather fitting. Operation Bodyguard and Operation Fortitude were code names for the misinformation campaign designed to trick the Germans into thinking the Allies were landing at a different time in a different place. The French Resistance operations to sabotage railways and roads and telephone lines included code names like Blue, Green, Purple, and Tortoise. The joint British and Canadian paratrooper landings just after midnight were code-named Operation Tonga. The name given to the beach invasion itself was Operation Neptune.

In the spirit of the code names the Allies gave to their operations, I've made up a few code names for some of my characters. Dee, Sid, Bill, Henry, and even Dorothy and Monique are all technically parts of the beach invasion, and therefore could all be considered to be carrying out facets of Operation Neptune. To make each of their stories more clearly separate, I invented the names Operation Amiens (Bill and *Achilles*), Operation Integration (Henry), and Operation Bathing Suit (Monique and Dorothy).

OPERATION NEPTUNE

Thanks in part to poor navigation, rough seas, and stronger-than-expected German defenses, the American landing on Omaha Beach was a disaster. Soldiers were delivered almost anywhere but where they were supposed to land, and most of the tank support that made the other beaches easier by comparison didn't arrive until much later in the day. Allied bombers, afraid of hitting their own men or being shot by German anti-aircraft guns, dropped their bombs well before their intended targets, and the battleships at sea, also afraid of return fire, didn't come in close enough to shore initially to do any real damage to the fortified German positions on the cliffs.

The invading soldiers were expected to be up and off the beach within three hours of landing—by nine thirty in the morning. In reality, most of the surviving American soldiers didn't make it off the beach until well after two o'clock in the afternoon. Even then, only a few of the planned routes up and off the beach were open by the end of the day. Things went so badly that the American commanders considered giving up on Omaha entirely and withdrawing any surviving soldiers. Of the more than 4,000 Allied soldiers who died on D-Day, almost half of that number were Americans who died on Omaha. By comparison, fewer than 200 American soldiers died on Utah Beach.

Many immigrants and foreign nationals served in the United States military during the Second World War, as Dee does here. More than 300,000 immigrants served in the US armed forces during the war, a third of them non-citizens.

Canada was slow to send its soldiers into a war so far from home, so many Canadians who wanted to fight joined the US military to see action right away. They were joined by tens of thousands of volunteers from Mexico, Germany, Italy, and dozens more countries—all of them with the common goal of defeating the Axis powers (Germany, Italy, and Japan). Many, like Dee, who were political dissidents from German-controlled countries, changed their names to avoid being executed or sent to concentration camps should they have been captured by the Nazis. And like Dee, almost all of them chose to become naturalized US citizens after the war. Immigrants and foreign nationals have fought for the United States in every major conflict since the American Revolution. Today there are more than half a million foreign-born veterans living in the United States, and close to 10,000 non-citizens enlist in the US military each year.

Like Sid, many Jewish soldiers who served in the United States military during the Second World War experienced anti-Semitism from their fellow soldiers and faced institutionalized prejudice when they returned home. During the war, prominent Americans like Henry Ford and Charles Lindbergh gave speeches and wrote articles blaming Jewish Americans for the US involvement in the war, and afterward, many restaurants, hotels, and shops continued to refuse to serve Jewish Americans. It wasn't until the Civil Rights Act of 1964 that the United States officially outlawed discrimination on the basis of race, color, religion, sex, or national origin.

OPERATION TORTOISE

The French Resistance's major contributions to the success of D-Day were intelligence and sabotage. French Resistance intelligence reports provided far more accurate troop strengths than aerial reconnaissance could, and rail lines were sabotaged to create enormous train wrecks and snarl long-distance travel for the Germans. The Resistance was also skilled at cutting phone and telegraph lines to prevent German communications. In addition to being disruptive, their sabotage efforts had other benefits for the Allies: Destroying rail lines forced the Germans to move their tanks by roadway, burning precious gasoline. And cutting phone lines made the Germans resort to communicating by radio, which the Allies could listen in on. The French Resistance was so effective at slowing transportation within their borders that one German army division took just one week to move all the way from Russia to the border of France—a distance of two thousand miles—but *three weeks* to go from the border of France to the city of Caen: a distance of less than 500 miles.

Like Samira and her mother, many Algerians fought on the side of France in both the Resistance and the army. In return for their contributions, French Algerians were promised independence. What they got instead, once the war was over, was the offer of French citizenship, not independence, angering many Algerians. A celebration in Algeria to mark the end of the war turned into a protest against French rule, and eighty-four European settlers were killed. The French army responded by killing thousands of Algerians. Known as the Sétif Massacre, the bloodshed on both sides sowed the seeds for the Algerian War of Independence that began nine years later. Algerians finally won their independence from France in 1962, but only after a long, bloody, bitter war.

OPERATION TONGA

Paratroopers at D-Day were often dropped miles from their targets. Many paratroopers drowned in the fields the Germans had flooded. Others were shot before they hit the ground. Sometimes paratroopers even came down on top of German defenses—literally. More than one paratrooper reported landing on the roof of a German barrack. Throughout the night, paratroopers from different companies came together and managed to achieve their many different goals, despite being undermanned and sometimes poorly armed.

The battle of Varaville Château was a real battle, although I fictionalized it here. A severely outmanned Canadian team forced the surrender of a much larger German garrison—much to the surprise and dismay of the Nazis once they saw how few there were of the enemy. The actual battle lasted until around ten thirty in the morning; I've compressed time a little here to have it end a bit sooner.

If Day was a real event too, held in Winnipeg, Manitoba, Canada, on February 19, 1942. The exhibition raised more than three million dollars for the Canadian war effort and was featured in the pages of *Life* magazine, *Newsweek*, and the *New York Times*. Since then, If Day has been the subject of a number of documentaries and television shows.

In Canada, Indigenous peoples, also known as First Nations, were long seen as second-class citizens by Canadian law. The 1951 Indian Act rescinded some of the more egregious restrictions on them, but still legalized many forms of discrimination. It wasn't until a 1985 law change that many Canadian First Nations regained tribal status that had been taken away from them over decades of discrimination. Though much amended and better for First Nations than it was originally, the Indian Act remains controversial.

OPERATION AMIENS

Thanks to innovations that allowed them to float, Sherman tanks played an important role in most of the Allied beach invasions. The one place they were *not* as effective was on Omaha Beach. Twenty-seven of the initial twenty-nine tanks meant to land on Omaha sank on their way in to shore.

British soldiers *did* drive American-made Sherman tanks—President Franklin Delano Roosevelt famously called the United States the "Arsenal of Democracy" due to America's leading role in producing arms for all its allies. I have no evidence that a British tank crew ever landed on Omaha Beach, but in an effort to show the contributions of all the major Allied players *and* connect them to my story, I've taken some historical license to have Bill and his *Achilles* crewmates end up on Omaha and play a small role in Dee's story.

If Bill had made it as far as Bayeux, he would not have found the Bayeux Tapestry there. During the Second World War, the tapestry resided in the Louvre, a famous museum in Paris, France. Eager to loot expensive works of art from museums and private collections all over Europe, Nazi leaders ordered local SS officers to steal the Bayeux Tapestry and other priceless pieces from the Louvre before abandoning Paris to the Allies in August 1944. The Nazis were foiled by the French Resistance, who intercepted and decoded the order and took control of the Louvre in time to defend it from Nazi soldiers when they came to take the art. Today the tapestry has returned home to Bayeux, where it is on display in a museum dedicated to the Bayeux Tapestry—and the Invasion of Normandy.

OPERATION INTEGRATION

The character of Henry Allen is based largely on Waverly "Woody" Woodson, a black army medic from Philadelphia who, like Henry, graduated from Officer Training School only to find that the United States Army was not interested in having black men become officers. Despite never expecting to see actual combat, Woodson and the rest of the 320th Barrage Balloon Battalion were delivered into the middle of a battle on Omaha Beach. Woodson worked tirelessly during D-Day, tending to wounded soldiers, black and white alike.

The 320th as a whole won a commendation from General Eisenhower for their extraordinary service on Omaha Beach. Woodson was one of four medics from the 320th who individually received a Bronze Star. Many years later, it was revealed that Woodson had been nominated for a Medal of Honor but was passed over for the award. A 1997 army inquiry found that institutional racism had kept many deserving black veterans of the Second World War from receiving the highest military honors. That same year, President Bill Clinton retroactively awarded Medals of Honor to seven African American soldiers who deserved the award for their actions during the war, but only one of them was still alive to accept his award in person. Waverly Woodson was, again, not among the seven men honored.

According to Linda Hervieux's *Forgotten*, a book about the black soldiers who fought at D-Day, approximately 1,800 African Americans took part in D-Day—most of them in support roles. After serving with distinction in the war, black American soldiers returned home to racism, prejudice, and persecution. White

German prisoners of war were treated better than black men who had served their own country during the war. The United States Army officially ended its policy of segregation in 1948, but the nation's schools were not integrated until the late 1950s. The civil rights movement, which reached its peak in the 1950s and 1960s in the United States, sought to end segregation and establish racial justice and equality in all parts of American society. Perhaps its greatest achievement was the Civil Rights Act of 1964, which outlawed any discrimination on the basis of race. Though the civil rights movement made great gains, the United States still struggles today with the same kind of racism and prejudice Henry faced seventy-five years ago.

OPERATION BATHING SUIT

French citizens who lived in the towns and villages of Normandy soon knew the Allied invasion was happening, and many of them rushed to the beaches to welcome their liberators and help in any way they could. One young French woman, a student nurse, really had left her bathing suit in a changing hut on the beach the day before, and rode her bicycle down to get it—just minutes before the first shots were fired. She ignored the catcalls and whistles of the soldiers on the beach and spent the next two days helping bandage up wounded men—including the English soldier who would later become her husband. I adapted her story here and made her much younger.

Dorothy Powell is based on the real-life reporter Martha Gellhorn, who disguised herself as a soldier to sneak ashore with a stretcher crew on D-Day. She was the first and only American woman to set foot on the beach at Normandy on June 6, 1944. It would be another thirty-eight days until the next American woman arrived, when forty-nine WACs—members of the Women's Army Corps, a support branch of the United States Army—stepped off landing boats into France. It would be another fifty years before American women were allowed to serve in actual combat.

A war correspondent for a number of magazines and newspapers over her long career, Gellhorn reported on every major war and conflict from the Second World War through the US invasion of Panama in 1989. Today, the Martha Gellhorn Prize for Journalism recognizes men and women who chronicle the lives of ordinary people caught up in violent conflicts.

BEYOND OMAHA BEACH

While a number of smaller towns and villages lay claim to the title of "First village liberated on D-Day," Bayeux was certainly the first French city freed by Allied soldiers. It was officially liberated on June 7, 1944, not June 6—I sped up Bayeux's liberation by a few hours to get all my players there before midnight, thus taking us from twelve a.m. to twelve a.m. and limiting the events in the book to a single day—D-Day.

The area just beyond the bunker I used as inspiration for the one Dee and Sid take when they first come up off Omaha Beach is now a graveyard and memorial to all the American soldiers who died on D-Day. The Normandy American Cemetery and Memorial is home to 9,380 graves and receives more than a million visitors each year.

ACKNOWLEDGMENTS

Like Dee at D-Day, I was helped by many allies in the writing of this book. Huge thanks to my ever-patient and always wise editor, Aimee Friedman; my publisher, David Levithan; copyeditor Jessica White and proofreaders Jody Corbett, Jackie Hornberger, and Bethany Bryan; and everyone else behind the scenes at Scholastic: Ellie Berger, president of Trade Publishing; Tracy van Straaten and Amy Goppert in Publicity; Mindy Stockfield, Rachel Feld, and Julia Eisler in Marketing; Lizette Serrano, Emily Heddleson, Michael Strouse, Matthew Poulter, Jasmine Miranda, and Danielle Yadao in School and Library Marketing and Conventions; Aimee's assistant editor, Olivia Valcarce; Josh Berlowitz, Elizabeth Krych, Erin O'Connor, Leslie Garych, Joanne Mojica, and everyone in Production; Yaffa Jaskoll and Stephanie Yang for the terrific cover and interior layout; map artist

Jim McMahon; Jazan Higgins, Stephanie Peitz, Jana Haussmann, Ann Marie Wong, Kristin Standley, Robin Hoffman, and everyone with the Clubs and Fairs; Jennifer Powell, Hillary Doyle, Bryan West, and Rachel Weinert in Rights and Co-Editions; Alan Smagler, Elizabeth Whiting, Jackie Rubin, Alexis Lunsford, Alexis Lassiter, Dan Moser, Nikki Mutch, Sue Flynn, Chris Satterlund, Roz Hilden, Terribeth Smith, Randy Kessler, Betsy Politi, Charlie Young, and everyone in Sales; Lori Benton, John Pels, and Paul Gagne for their amazing work, as ever, on *Allies* the audiobook; and all the sales reps and Fairs and Clubs reps across the country who work so hard to tell the world about my books.

Thank you to Trent Reedy and Linda Hervieux, who read my manuscript and gave me notes. Your comments were invaluable, and any mistakes that remain are my own. Thanks as always to my great friend Bob. And big thanks to my literary agent, Holly Root at Root Literary, and to my publicists and right-hand women Lauren Harr and Caroline Christopoulos at Gold Leaf Literary—the work you do allows me to do the work *I* do. And thanks again to all the teachers, librarians, and booksellers out there who put my books into the hands of young readers—you're awesome! And last but never least, much love and thanks to my wife, Wendi, and my daughter, Jo.

We are stronger together.

ABOUT THE AUTHOR

Alan Gratz is the *New York Times* bestselling author of several acclaimed books for young readers, including *Refugee*, a New York Times Notable Book and an Amazon, Kirkus Reviews, and Publishers Weekly Best Book of the Year; *Grenade*, the 2018 Freeman Book Award winner; *Projekt 1065*, a Kirkus Reviews Best Book of the Year; *Prisoner B-3087*, winner of eight state awards and included on YALSA's 2014 Best Fiction for Young Adults list; and *Code of Honor*, a YALSA 2016 Quick Pick for Reluctant Young Adult Readers. Alan lives in North Carolina with his wife and daughter. Look for him online at alangratz.com.